Karoo Boy

KAROO BOY

Troy Blacklaws

A HARVEST ORIGINAL

HARCOURT, INC.

Orlando   Austin   New York   San Diego   Toronto   London

© 2004 Troy Blacklaws

All rights reserved. No part of this publication may be reproduced or transmitted in any form or by any means, electronic or mechanical, including photocopy, recording, or any information storage and retrieval system, without permission in writing from the publisher.

Requests for permission to make copies of any part of the work should be mailed to the following address: Permissions Department, Harcourt, Inc., 6277 Sea Harbor Drive, Orlando, Florida 32887-6777.

www.HarcourtBooks.com

First published in South Africa by Double Storey Books in 2004

Library of Congress Cataloging-in-Publication Data
Blacklaws, Troy.
Karoo boy/Troy Blacklaws.—1st U.S. edition.
"A Harvest Original."
p. cm.
1. Twins—Fiction.   2. Death—Fiction.   3. Karoo (South Africa)—Fiction.
4. South Africa—Fiction.   I. Title.
PR9369.4.B57K37   2005
823'.92—dc22   2005046392
ISBN-13: 978-0156-03065-6   ISBN-10: 0-15-603065-9

Text set in Minion

Printed in the United States of America

First U.S. edition 2005
K J I H G F E D C B A

This is a work of fiction. Names, characters, places, organizations, and events are the products of the author's imagination or are used fictitiously, and any resemblance to actual persons, living or dead, events, or locales is entirely coincidental.

For Finn-Christian, who loves stories

KAROO BOY

seagulls

Christmas day 1976 in Muizenberg, Cape Town. The midday sun blazes down. The air smells of coconut suntan oil and ribs on the braai. Smoke drifts up to cawing, squalling seagulls in the sky. On the tyre-hardened earth, between the tar road and the sand of Sunrise Beach, we Thomas men and boys play cricket barefoot. The earth under me is piping hot, and I rock from heel to toe, toe to heel.

My father is bowling. He rubs the leather ball against his bermudas, so it will swing in the air. He loves cricket and has high hopes that one of his boys, Marsden or me, will play cricket for the province one day.

I field on the far fringe of the parking lot. A sand yacht glides between me and the tomato-box wicket, risking the bone-hard ball.

Bulky Oom Jan, my winefarmer uncle from over the Simons-berg, turns the ribs on the braai with one hand and then licks the fat off his fingers. In the other hand he holds a dumpie of Lion Lager. If the fire jumps too high he douses it with a shake of beer.

The women lie on beach towels in the sand under the shade of wind-rippling umbrellas. The girls skip over waves at the water's edge, or float on lilos.

I can see my mother's red bikini and her butterfly sunglasses. I know she is biting the inside of her lip as she reads, and is dreaming of having her feet tickled, or of a drop of Tabasco on an oyster, or of plucking a periwinkle from a rock and sucking it out raw.

My twin brother, Marsden, lies in the shade with my mother, sketching. My mother sometimes calls him her little Picasso. He has an art scholarship for all his high school years, but the folks have to fork out the fees for me.

My mother just calls me Dee, although my name is Douglas. Douglas James Thomas.

My mother glances up from her book to wave at me. I wave back, wishing I was free to go in search of a periwinkle for my mother, but they are hard to find. You have to go up the east coast as far as Hermanus to find clusters of shellfish on the rocks. Oom Jan says it is the bloody coloureds who plunder the rocks. My father says it is the Transvalers from up north, Johannesburg way, who come down and ransack the Cape.

My eyes drift. If you want to be a journalist, my father often tells me, you need to have an eye for detail.

Behind me, coloured fruitsellers, sheltering from the sun under makeshift tents of canvas, call out their fruits: liiichis banaaanas avocaaados.

A coloured fisherman dodges motorcars on the road, jiggling his catch of snoek, a fish as long and speary as a barracuda.

– Hout Bay snoek, Hout Bay snoek, jus' a rand, he raps to the motorcars.

Just one rand for a barracuda-long snoek, for a taste of heaven when braaied in a dip of apricot jam, the way my father does it.

Some folk slow down to squint at the snoek. Others hit the

gas as if to run the fisherman down. He skips aside, the way a mongoose jumps clear of darting snake fangs.

The ball bounces past me onto the tar road. I dash after it and a Ford bakkie full of jeering Transvalers hoots at me. A beer can clatters and spins across the tar, as if shot by a cowboy.

I throw the ball back to my father, hoping it will reach him without a bounce. The breeze coming off the sea pulls it down, short. I can tell by the jerky way my father rubs the ball against his bermudas that he is cross that my mind was not on the game. Then he bowls out cousin Dirkie, Oom Jan's boy, splintering the tomato-box wicket. My father is smiling again.

We have all had a chance to bat, so my father calls Marsden, still sketching seagulls in the shade. He wants to stay in the shade, but my father and uncles and boy cousins taunt him until he drops his pencils in the sand. His rice paper blows away in the wind. Beyond the girls and the breakers, windsurfers plane across the bay. A hang-glider loops in the azure sky.

Dirkie, all sour-faced because he was bowled out, chucks my brother the bat. It is a Gunn & Moore willowwood bat. I have often sat out on the stoep in the evenings when the sun sinks behind the Muizenberg mountain, rubbing linseed oil into the wood. I love the smell of the oil and the wood.

Marsden looks around to get a sense of where the gaps are and then taps the foot of the bat in the sand. To anyone other than my mother or father, it could be me, bat in hand. To the onlooker, Marsden and I are xeroxed, one like the other.

Over the sound of the surf, the cawing of gulls, and the rev and hum of motorcars on the road out to Stellenbosch, I hear the bell of a lollyboy on a bicycle. I would love a granadilla ice with the black pips that catch in your teeth so you have to fiddle them out with your tongue.

I watch my father run up and let the ball go early so that it arcs high. For a moment it is lost in the white glare of the sun, and then I catch sight of it again just as it curves down towards my brother. I think he is fooling because he takes a wild swipe at it that spins him around. I hear a dull thud, like a swallow flying into a windowpane. My brother drops to the sand. His face is out of focus in the mirage haze dancing on the sand.

I hear my father's raw cry and the earth goes wavy under my feet. My father runs to Marsden. He lifts my brother up in his arms, the way he carries firewood. He walks down to the sea, past the women who have abandoned umbrellas to clasp gog-eyed children. My brother's head flops as my father's feet sink into the beach sand.

My mother darts across the sand and clutches at my brother. But my father won't let him go. He spins away from her and my mother's nails scratch down his back.

My mother's cries are a skyful of gaping-beaked seagulls.

My father wades into the water until the waves break against him and wash over my brother. My brother's head lolls and my heart soars because the sea has revived him. But no, it is just the lilt of the wave that lifts his head, as if it were kelp on a rock.

Then I cannot see again, because my mother holds me against her cheek. The taste of her salt tears makes me cry.

My father is out deep with my brother, like a fisherman being pulled out by a hooked shark. Oom Jan wades in to drag him back to the beach.

Dirkie gawks at me. I smell the ribs on Oom Jan's braai burn.

Bent over my brother, my father sinks to his knees in the sand. He turns to face us. There is something wild in his eyes.

My mother's gaze is hard. I can see the bone in her cheek stand out.

coral seeds

A sugarbird's wings blur above pink hibiscus. My mother comes through the gate of our house on the edge of the Zandvlei lagoon. The bird flies over the fence, to Bessie Malan's yard. My mother lugs a cardboard box of books and things. It says *Cape* on the box because such boxes are used to export Cape fruit overseas.

– Dee, I have given up my teaching post, she says.

Given up after fifteen years of teaching history to high-school kids. Teaching them Blood River and Dingaan and Rhodes and the Boer War.

I wonder how things will go on from here. Marsden is gone. My father no longer taps away at his typewriter in his study in the yard. My mother is never going to come home again with chalk on her hands, or foolscap papers to stain with rooibos tea and red ink.

My mother drops the box on the pine floorboards that Hope, our Xhosa maid, waxes on her hands and knees with Cobra wax.

Hope is kipping outside in her backyard khaya. I hear her woodsawing snores. She is always saying that it is too shushu out there, with the sun beating down on the zinc roof. Before she has her afternoon kip she hoses down the roof with cold water.

Inside the house, under a thatched roof, it is cool.

– I want to turn the front room into a studio. I want to clear a space in this clutter, my mother says.

She heads for the front room that overlooks the lagoon. If she wants space, why not empty out Marsden's room? On his window sill: Tennessee, the tortoise, and a jar of porcupine quills and guineafowl feathers from Oom Jan's farm. Another jar just of paintbrushes. The big art books rippled by the dank sea air: Picasso and Miro and Matisse. The yellowwood box full of his sketches and paintings of Kalk Bay fishing boats, of seagulls, of Greenmarket Square, and of me.

Marsden once said to me, on the train to school: being a twin is being free to draw self-portraits without looking in a mirror.

For me, being a twin was having another boy on hand to throw a cricket ball to, to surf with, another mind for my thoughts to mingle with, and peel away from again, coloured by his. It was the feeling of being moored to another soul.

– Douglas, give me a hand, my mother calls.

In each hand she holds a tall lamp stand made from a Masai spear, from the twinless days when my mother and father lived in Kenya. She goes out, toting the spears as if she is on the warpath.

I pick up the hollow elephant-foot stool in which Nana, my grandmother, stored her balls of wool. As I go down the kitchen steps, Hope peeks her dozy-tortoise head out of her khaya window. She has forgotten to tie her spongy hair down in her doek. I giggle at Hope: hair undoeked and eyes agog.

I put the stool down under the shade of the coral tree. It used to be a kaffirboom, but the word *kaffir* is a rude word for blacks, so you may not call it a kaffirboom nowadays. Hope still calls it a kaffirboom, but she is black, so that is okay.

I tip up the lid of the elephant-foot stool to see colourful eggs of wool laid by an exotic bird.

Byron, the Xhosa gardenboy, abandons his digging to carry the armchairs across the kikuyu grass to the street kerb.

An old coloured man watches us from the edge of the lagoon. Perhaps he thinks: White folks are crazy. Before my eyes, a madam and her boy chuck good things out onto the street.

The debris from our front room gathers on the kerb, under the shade of the coral tree. There is the Morris chair my father tilts back to read the *Cape Times*. There is my dead grandmother Nana's Singer sewing-machine. There my dead grandfather Dodi's bentwood chairs from England.

My grandfather Dodi keeled over in a betting shop, after putting mucho money on the horse Jamaica. Jamaica was ahead when Dodi gasped and tipped forward, the beer glass slicing a half-moon in his forehead. Nana got the money Jamaica won for Dodi. She called it blood money. She split it for Marsden and me to inherit. Then she pined to death for him.

My father will not mind all the flotsam on the kerb. Nowadays he just goes from his outside study to the kitchen to cut himself a slice of bread, and back to his study. He never glances into Marsden's room, or detours into mine. He pees outside, under the frangipani. He goes to bed long after my mother and I fall asleep. I see his rippled sheets in the morning. When he is in his study, he stares at the postcard of the Venus de Milo on the wall, and does not sense me at the door. I have to knock to get him to swivel his chair.

Still jammed in his typewriter are the words he wrote over a fortnight ago, just before we went down to the beach on Christmas day, on how the magic of the sangoma, the witchdoctor, survives in the townships, so far from the Transkei.

When the bones rattle in the sangoma's hands, you instinctively
What do you instinctively do? Instinctively hold your breath? Instinctively believe?

Hope, in a hibiscus-pink pinafore, huffs past me. She has rescued Nana's Singer from under the coral and drags it into the dim of her khaya, where the sun mirages on the zinc roof.

I peer into the murky khaya. Before my eyes focus, smells of Vaseline and Lifebuoy waft to me. Out of a frame on the news-papered box by her bed, her boy September peeks at me. He lives in Peddie in the Ciskei with Hope's folks because Hope does not want him running around the townships like a footloose Langa skollie, a wild gangboy. No, she wants her September to learn the old ways.

Hope always tells us stories she hears from other maids: of old township folk baited by the skollies for bowing their heads to the whites all their life long. The old ones cower. For the young ones it is a joke. Hope rolls her eyes, as if to say this country is going downhill.

There is no school for black boys in Muizenberg, where Hope could keep an eye on September. So he stays up there in dusty Peddie. Hope sees him at Christmas when she rides the bus all the way up the Indian Ocean coast, through Port Elizabeth and Grahamstown, to Peddie. She says the ride is hell, as the bus is crowded and hot and slow. She always gives September a box of hand-me-downs from Marsden and me. Now there will be no castoffs from Marsden.

Everything is gone from the front room but the orange corduroy sofa, alone in the corner. The sofa is from the sixties when my mother and father came to the Cape from Kenya. Above the sofa is the ghost shape on the wall where the fake Dali hung: a clock melting under the desert sun. Under the sofa are the photo albums.

– If the house goes up in flames, my mother would say after a glass of red wine, rescue the photos, everything else can burn.

The sun floods in through the windows, as even the blinds have gone.

– Hey bro', I say into the dust-dancing emptiness, and I think I hear my brother's voice in the ripple of an echo.

My mother comes into the room and I swing around, wondering if she heard me.

– I am going to sleep on the sofa, my mother says.

What she means is that she is not going to sleep in the same bed as my father. I know she wants to let him suffer. I want to shout out: It was an accident. But I am scared of my mother's new-found vigour, the way she briskly crosses the yard and calls:

– Come on, Dee, don't just stand there in a daze.

I have a habit of standing in a daze. Whenever I play tennis doubles I stand at the net and the ball flies down the trams because I daydream.

Measure the net, a racquet, a head and two fingers (two fingers: same as the measure for my father's Jack Daniel's Tennessee whiskey). Spin for serve. Rough or smooth? Marsden and I spin a coin for who serves into the sun.

I stand around. I am not much help.

Chaka barks at the inside things outside. What a game, the flowing of our world out onto the kerb. He cocks his leg to pee against a Masai lamp stand but my mother gives him a kick in the ribs. Chaka yelps and darts back into the yard. Out of sheer shame he drags his ass along the grass.

This fazes me. I have never seen my mother hurt an animal before. Mossies land on her hands to peck seed, and goldfish swim through her seaweed fingers. She forbids Hope to flyswat the lizard-eating spider in the pantry. She forbade Marsden and me to shoot mossies, even though they are two a penny. When we shot pigeons on Oom Jan's farm we hid them from her.

You can tell she is sorry, for she lets the blinds clatter to the kerb and calls Chaka to her. He slinks along the yard wall. No way I'll risk another rib kick, he thinks. But he gives in to her calls, as dogs do, and she hugs him, the half-boxer, half-godknowswhat she picked out of a cage of bony, yipping pups at the dog pound.

Chaka licks her face and then spins around after his tail, which he will never catch, as it is docked. Fool dog chasing a lopped tail.

Then my mother comes over to me. She hugs me too and Hope melts at the kitchen door as tears fill my eyes.

– Oh Dee, life has gone all sour, my mother says to me.

Sour as milk left in the sun.

I begin to cry hard for Marsden dead and gone, and love gone too. But my tears turn to laughter because Chaka dances a giddy dance on the grass, biting at the wind. Crazy bobtail dog, always barking at seagulls and at the coloureds who walk by.

The old coloured man by the lagoon is still watching us, thinking maybe: What a carry-on for folks with a big brick house and grass yard and blackmama maid.

He wanders off with a Masai lamp stand in hand. It looks like the parasols the coloureds carry down Adderley Street during the Coon Carnival. Lips and eyes painted white and wide like the lips and eyes of a clown. Parasols jousting at the sky to the beat of the song that goes: *My geliefde hang in die bos, my geliefde hang in die bos, my gelieeefde hang in die bitterbessiebos.*

My love hangs in the bitterberry bush. The love of my mother for my father hangs in the bitterberry bush. It is as dead as a lizard spiked on a thorn by a butcher bird. It died when the ball hit my brother's head.

I pick up black-eyed, orange seeds from under the coral tree, among the tumbling relics of our front room. I pocket them because my father, teller of myths, told me they are juju seeds, they bring good luck.

— I want you to go back to school tomorrow, my mother says.

I do not want to ride the train without spinning a coin with Marsden for the window seat. I do not want the boys at school staring at me, the undead twin. But then I remember Mister Skinner, who coaches cricket. We schoolboys call him Skin for short. I know Skin will look into my eyes and say:

— Douglas, I'm sorry your brother is dead.

The other teachers will cast sorrowful glances at me and go on as if nothing has changed. I know this because of the time Drew Castle's mother died when a tossed stone flew through her windshield. Skin was the only teacher who went up to him and looked Drew in the eyes and said: I'm sorry.

Cape Town is an unafrican Africa where spears turn into lamp stands, and elephants into foot stools. An Africa of dogs and cats and garden gnomes. Death catches you off guard, lulled by the tunes of Radio 5, or playing cricket on the beach.

So, I will go to school again. I finger the juju seeds of the coral, hoping they will ward death away from me.

I walk down along the Zandvlei lagoon as the sun falls behind the Muizenberg mountain, then jaywalk across the Strandfontein road, jumping a gap in the motorcars that bead along the tar.

The fisherman who sold fish on Christmas day is still dangling snoek and dodging motorcars, jaunty and cocky as ever.

The sea wind sweeps high-tide sand across the road.

On the far side of the half-moon bay the dying sun stains the Hottentots Holland Mountains a rusty orange. Coloured fishermen beach their nets beyond Sunrise Beach, but my father is not there among the flocking seagulls and the fish flipping over like bluegum leaves in a breeze.

I walk on the beach, past the lemon and pink and sky-blue cabins.

There is my father, on the rocks where the beach runs out and the surfers ride the dusk tide. Above the rocks is the railway that snakes along the shore to Simonstown through St James, Kalk Bay, Clovelly and Fish Hoek. My father gazes out to sea, still as a cormorant watching the rock pools for a flicker of fish.

He senses me near him. For a moment there is the old spark in his eyes, as if I may just be my brother and it was all a dream. But he sees it is me and, in seeing me, sees the boy he killed. His eyes swivel out to sea again. He combs his fingers through my hair, but it is not long before his hand goes limp on my head. I know that he is somewhere out there beyond the surfers, beyond Seal Island. I want to call him back but all I do is stare at my feet in the rock pool, at the way the water warps my feet so they jut out skew from the end of my legs.

As I stare, a face falls into focus and Marsden stares back at me.

– Douglas, I am going away.

I flinch. The face in the water fades. An empty black mussel gapes at my toes.

– Where will you go?

– I'm not sure. Maybe east.

I see my father sailing east along the coast as far as Malindi, where Bo Hansen will put him up. Maybe he will pick up the novel he began when he and my mother lived in Kenya. He always dreamed of being an author, but with Marsden and me on his hands he never had the time to write for himself, just for the paper.

When Marsden and I were nine my father was sent to London for a year by the *Cape Times* to report on the hippies who stood

outside South Africa House in Trafalgar Square, chanting for freedom in South Africa. We lived in Camden, close to the zoo and
Camden Market and the reggae-coloured barges on the canal.
But when I think of England, I always think of the sun-flared day
when we rowed on the river at Hampton.

My father at the oars of the skiff, Marsden and I trailing our
hands in the green water. No fear of sharks, just ducks and swans to
throw stale bread to.

Then we came to Muizenberg, to the house on the lagoon, six
thousand miles south of Camden. Every day for years my father
railed into the city to edit on the news desk. Then, a year ago,
when Soweto fired up, he gave up editing to freelance. He wrote
about the gangs in the townships, about the bergies, down-and-
outs who camp under canvas or tattered beach umbrellas on the
mountain slopes, about the hobos who kip under newspaper in
parks, maybe kipping under my father's stories.

And he wrote about the Crossroads squatters. One time,
Marsden and I went along to Crossroads shantytown with my
father. He wanted to photograph the police bulldozing down the
shacks. I saw mothers gather their world in bags and give their
children rubbery chicken feet to gnaw on. I saw men jab futile fists
at the police. I saw shacks tumble down under bulldozers.

Though my father was forever out hunting stories or typing
them up in his study, on Saturdays he was free to watch Marsden
and me play cricket. When we played in the Boland he drove us
out there in the grey tailfinned Benz: Indlovu, Xhosa for elephant.

Indlovu rusts in the salty wind, but my father always loved
her. He rode her with one hand on the wheel, whistling the tunes
on Radio 5.

Coasting along the Strandfontein road to Stellenbosch: the sun
glinting on the Benz star up front, cool salty wind rivers in, my

father taps a beat on the dashboard with his fingertips. Creedence
Clearwater or Fleetwood Mac or The Beach Boys floating out the
windows, mingling with the smell of the sea.

Feet in a rock pool. Limp hand on my head. No music floating
out to sea. Just my father and I, so still a sandpiper flits by a few
feet away. It halts, wagtails for a moment, and then flits on again.

– Who will watch me play cricket?

I wonder if he still dreams of me playing for the province. I
spend most summer afternoons after school caged in the cricket
nets while others surf or cruise the downtown cafés or go to the
flicks in Rondebosch. I am good at batting but when I field, my
eyes drift, and I gaze up at Table Mountain, some days moody
grey, some days tinted the ochre of fired clay. My mind is not
focused enough for me to make it in cricket.

– From now on you have to play for yourself, Douglas.

A stone's throw away a coloured man catches an octopus
among the rocks. He holds it up to the sky and it ropes around
his arm. With a flick, he turns it inside out and dashes it down on
the rocks. He gathers the squirming jelly fronds and flings it down
again and again to pulp its rubber flesh.

– I have something for you.

In his hand is his Zippo lighter and his Swiss Army pocket
knife. Marsden and I always fought over who would get the Zippo
and who the pocket knife when my father thought us old enough
for knives and fire.

– You're a big boy, Douglas.

I had always imagined I would be over the moon if he ever
gave either to me, but I just pocket them. I stare out to sea and
recall the myth my father told Marsden and me on the Kalk Bay
harbour wall, of how love came out of the sea.

The blood of Zeus dripped into the deep water beyond the break-

ers and mingled with the sea foam, and Venus was born. Dolphins fed her and held sharks at bay. When she was a woman with mango breasts, she waded ashore onto the sliver of beach in Kalk Bay harbour and sent the Kalk Bay whalers so crazy with longing they flung themselves from Skeleton Rock.

Now Venus has gone back to the sea, among kelp lilting dark as shark shadows.

red bait

The cold bay wind gnaws at my cheeks as I stand on the Valsbaai platform, waiting for the train from Simonstown.

Schoolboys in uniform play football with a tennis ball, scuffing their school shoes. Schoolgirls hold on to their wind-tugged skirts above bare knees and short white socks and black Bata sandals.

The girls think the boys are childish, chasing a ball across the platform. The boys are glad they do not have skirts that blow up in the wind so they are free to chase a ball. The boys and girls sometimes glance at me, standing alone in the cold wind. No doubt they think: There's Douglas. Him with the dead twin.

But they glance away guiltily when I catch their eye.

Businessmen try to catch their *Cape Times* from blowing away across the tracks.

SOWETO SCHOOLS BURN, the headlines cry.

There is a photo of a building in flames and the black gutted carcass of a bus in the foreground with schoolchildren dancing around it. In the distance you can make out the army trucks. The guns of the soldiers on the back of the trucks aim up at the sky, like the legs of a flipped-over insect.

The back page says there is a rumour of a rugby tour by the

Pumas of Argentina. The All Blacks and the Lions do not want to play the Springboks, because of apartheid. Oom Jan says it's because they are scared of being buggered up by the Springboks again.

At the level crossing the boom swings down and the motorcars jam.

I want to jump the tracks and catch a train going the other way, away from Rondebosch, away from school. Get off at Kalk Bay and dangle red bait to catch fish from the harbour wall.

The train comes into sight.

There is a scrambling for rucksacks and sport bags. A girl struggles with a guitar and sports gear and school books:

– Can I carry something for you? I offer.

Her cheeks tint.

– Okay, she says, and swings me her rucksack.

It is heavy. Full of biology and history books, no doubt.

– Grazie, she says as the train jolts on. I'll see you, hey.

She goes to join other girls and I hear them call her Marta.

Marta, with her ginger hair twisted into pigtails, makes my head fizz. I wish she would sit beside me to fill out, colour in the gaping hole of Marsden gone. But she abandons me to the emptiness I border on, giving all the colour and life of her to the other girls. Her pigtails flick like flywhisks when she swings her head.

My cheek against the cold glass, I see the world through a zoom lens: foreground of yards and dogs and bicycles in a blur, and Table Mountain in focus. Without a jostle for the window seat there is no fun in it. My rucksack, on the seat beside me, does not mind not having a view, never nudges, never rubs against me.

I fish the dog-eared copy of *The Old Man and the Sea* out of my blazer pocket. Miss Forster, my English teacher from last year in standard six, gave it to me. Miss Forster who wore frocks so summery you could see the curve of her breasts when she stood by the window. Now she has gone to Amsterdam for good. Oom Jan says the whites who voetsak overseas are cowards. They suck the fruit of the land while it is sweet and then, when it turns bitter, they run. My father says exile is a hard road. They do not waltz off to London and Amsterdam and Tasmania on a whim. But Oom Jan snorts, and downs another long sluk of Lion Lager. Anyway, it is better that those who do not love South Africa go, Oom Jan reckons. My father says he should be open-minded. Just because you leave something behind does not mean you do not love it. Oom Jan says it is the folk with a British passport in the back pocket who are so open-minded, as they know they can bugger off when the pawpaw hits the fan. And so it goes.

The Old Man and the Sea: Old man Santiago dreams of Africa, of white beaches and roaring surf. He tells the boy he has seen lions on the beach at dusk.

Maybe in Malindi or somewhere up the coast of East Africa you will see a lion on the beach, but in the Cape the lions have been hunted dead.

In his dreams Santiago smells the smell of Africa.

I wonder if he smells reeking kelp carried on the sea wind or the stink of snoek in the sun or the tang of bluegum or the dust snuff of a dirt road.

☞

The school, a private school, is shaded by stone pines and islanded by a sea of fields. Among all the white boys are a handful of Indians, blacks and coloureds. This is why Marsden and I were sent here, instead of going to the all-white government school in Muizenberg. My father wants us to grow up colour-blind. Oom Jan says the kind of fancy black boys pussyfooting across the cricket pitch at a private school are not the same as the barefoot black boys on the farm, just as he says American negroes like Muhammad Ali are not the same as your African black.

To skip the awkwardness of hanging around amid whispers and glances, I hide behind the cricket nets till the bell goes. *The Old Man and the Sea* is falling apart from being carted around in my pocket. I open it at random and read for the mood and echo of Miss Forster's voice. The school bell calls me back from the faraway sea where sharks strip the old man's fish to the bone. I have lost track of time. The timetable I was sent in the post says I have Mister Jansen, the history teacher, known for beating the hell out of the standard sevens because the sevens are always up to all sorts of high jinks.

I arrive breathless at Mister Jansen's door, expecting him to yell, but he just flashes his tobacco-yellowed teeth at me.

– You must be Douglas.

He does not offer a word on Marsden. He just hands me my book and bids me to a desk right under his nose. His eyebrows are paintbrushes of hog hair.

The boys cast their eyes down at pencilled textbooks but risk staring at me when he turns to chalk the blackboard again. I wish I was handlining for fish in Kalk Bay or visiting Miss Forster in Amsterdam.

I walk down a shadowy alley in Amsterdam. In the pink light of a window I glimpse a red garter against white skin, before my father's hand tugs at mine.

In my dreams it is Miss Forster dangling red bait in the shadows.

☞

When the bell goes I am sucked into a river of schoolboys. I catch Marsden's name, a float bobbing on the surface of a tumbling tide. Oliver weaves towards me, against the flow.

– Hey, Douglas, there's a cool karate flick on in town. A few of us are going Friday if you wanna come.

I know it is his way of saying sorry about Marsden.

– Sorry. My mother doesn't want me railing back out to Muizenberg after dark.

My mother does not want me to see karate flicks either. But this I do not tell him.

– Pity, says Oliver.

I get the feeling he is relieved.

The next class is with Skin. Though I know him from cricket, I have not yet been taught by him. He does not even glance at me, as if I have not missed a thing. As if he has not heard. He settles the class and says we have to read *The Great Gatsby*, while he plays a jazz record in the background. I do not have the book yet so he says I should go with him to the book room and I follow him.

The book room is a naked bulb and books stacked to the roof. I make out a few titles: *Catcher in the Rye*, *The Great Gatsby*, *To Kill a Mockingbird*, *Of Mice and Men*.

He dusts a copy of *The Great Gatsby* against his cords, and hands it to me.

– Douglas, I was dreadfully sorry to hear about your brother.

I stare at the dust smear on his cords as tears well in my eyes.

– I'll miss Marsden on the cricket pitch. But I hope you'll play on, in spite of everything.

– I want to play on, I sob.

My tears fall on to the cover of *The Great Gatsby*, a fiery tiger-skin pattern.

I mop the tears away with my sleeve.

– I am sorry about the book, I say.

And Skin reaches his arms out and holds me and I cry. His shirt is all wet with my crying. I want to cry against his shirt forever but part of me is ashamed about the shirt.

– Look, why don't we take a drive down to Sea Point after cricket. We'll see the sun go down from the Hard Rock, then I'll drive you home.

– To Muizenberg? It's far.

– We'll go via Hout Bay. I love the climb over Chapman's Peak.

– I don't have my cricket togs along.

– You could catch up with *Gatsby* in the library, or watch the practice.

– Okay, I nod.

– Good lad. Give your mother a bell, so she knows you're with me.

blue grass

The library is haunted by Old Shuttlecock, who stocks it up with books on Hitler and submarines. He is forever scuttling to the boys' john, keys a-jingle, to run the keys under a tap. Then he swings them on their string till they dry. He scares the hell out of schoolboys with his jangling keys, and he resents lending out books to savages like us. Still, I risk running into the war-crazed Old Shuttlecock rather than have the boys gawk at me through the nets.

From a dark corner of the library I hear the distant crack of cricket balls against wood.

I open *The Great Gatsby* at random. Lines underlined in a wavy freehand catch my eye. I read of blue grass and yellow cocktail music and the earth lurching away from the sun.

When the ball stoned Marsden's head, just in front of his earhole, I had the feeling the earth jerked away from the sun.

Now the earth floats unanchored in space.

– Come on then, Skin calls.

He is in his cricket whites. His hair is ruffled and his pants are stained red from rubbing the ball.

I pack the book into my rucksack and follow him out into the schoolyard. Oliver stands by a tap with a cluster of other boys who are splashing their faces and laughing. The laughter fades out as Skin and I go by. They look at their shoes and murmur to the teacher: 'noon, sir.

– Afternoon, boys, says Skin.

I can tell by the jaunty skip of his walk that he loves being the schoolmaster, being called sir.

– So, how'd you get on with *Gatsby*? Skin wants to know.

– I just dipped into the story, I tell him, conscious of the boys' eyes on us as we follow the curve of the cricket pitch to where his sky-blue Peugeot convertible is parked under the stone pines.

A flicker of feeling, maybe hurt, crosses his face.

– You need to give it time, he says.

For a moment, I am not sure if he means *Gatsby* or Marsden. But he goes on:

– His writing is magic, you know. You really get a sense of the time, the jazzy, feathered flamboyance of it all.

– I felt it a bit, I say, knowing teachers get wound up about the things they teach.

I recall a line about girls gliding through a sea-change of faces and I want to say something about the gliding but I am not sure I understand it. Instead, I remark:

– I liked the yellow music.

– Oh. You picked up on that? That's one of the magic things Fitzgerald does. Mixes the senses, so you hear colours and see sound.

It makes sense to me, as the sea smells turquoise, and red is the sound of a tomtom drummed by blurred hands.

Skin is happy about the yellow music, and he begins to whistle as he fishes for keys in his red-stained pocket. Behind me I hear the laughter of the boys pick up again.

Just as my father would, he spits in his handkerchief and wipes insect flecks from the windshield. Yellow flecks like flicks of a paintbrush. Then he draws the hood back and we climb inside.

~

We drive along De Waal Drive under Table Mountain, the distant cablecar house on the flat top like a tickbird riding a hippo's back. I look down on the scar of District Six, the skysigns of the city, and the cranes and masts of the harbour beyond.

Skin scratches through a cubbyhole full of boxless tapes.

– Ever heard of Miles Davis?

I know he is the jazzgod. My father would sometimes listen to jazz at night when he was writing: the tapping of his typewriter blending with the tinny tunes and the zinging of crickets and the far, fuzzy hiss of the surf. But I say no to Skin, as I sense he wants to feel he is initiating me into jazz. He fiddles with the dials and the music comes like a wave. I imagine the seals in the harbour far below tossing their heads towards the mountain and the sinking sun to catch the swooping sound.

Along Orange Street squirrel palms fountain green against the brick and tar. Then we glide downhill on Buitengracht, past steep, cobbled BoKaap Streets: Church, Bloem, Pepper, Leeuwen. The Moslem BoKaap: glimpses of giddy houses, a Malay mosque props up a blue sky, virgins' eyes hide behind black mosquito veils and the milky beards of old men flow into white cloth that drops from chin to sandal. From up here lions once gazed down on herds of zebra and straying Hottentot cows.

We jika into Strand Street. Under a date palm, a coloured man sells aeroplanes and windmills made out of wire and Coca-Cola cans. He stares toothlessly at us, as if Miles Davis is riding in the back seat with his trumpet tilted at the sky. We curve around the foot of Signal Hill and then drop down to the sea at Three Anchor Bay and ride on Beach Road, past Boat Bay, to Sea Point.

All the world is out jogging or cycling, or just perching on the railings to squint at the sinking sun while seagulls coast above the rocks. A young black man on roller skates weaves through a row of Coca-Cola cans, dodging skipperke dogs and bitterlemon lips pursing out from under straw hats. You can tell the dogwalkers think: This black is too cocky. Does he think he's on Venice Beach or something?

There is a lucky gap in the parking bay just this side of the Hard Rock. Miles chokes out. A black man in khaki shorts and an unbuttoned, flapping shirt jogs up to us.

– Hey chief, can I wash your car, chief? he goes.

– What the heck, alright. But mind you don't scratch the paint, says Skin.

– Sure chief, goes the washerman, all teeth.

His whistle stabs my eardrum and an old man comes hobbling up behind a Spar trolley. In the trolley are two buckets of murky water.

A pink Chevy has skydived into the roof of the Hard Rock. We weave through empty chairs and the upbeat vibe of *Pretty Flamingo*. The song is on one of my father's sixties mixes. Marilyn's skirt flicks up in a whisk of wind, the way skirts do when the southeaster gusts down Adderley Street.

The balcony is full but two girls shift up. One shades a

strawberry milkshake under spinnaker breasts. The freckled skin of the other girl is peeling on her shoulders. She pinches away a film of skin and chews it as we sit down.

Skin orders a Castle Lager. I go for a Coke float: two scoops of vanilla in a glass of Coca-Cola. The fizz makes the ice-cream froth like dirty sea foam.

Pretty Flamingo fades out and I instinctively wait for Cliff Richard to sing *Living Doll*, the way he does on my father's mix. But the hippy grooves of *San Francisco* flow instead.

– When you go to San Franciscooo, Skin croons along.

The girls giggle at him, but he does not hear them.

– Ah, this revives my student days in London, goes Skin, squeezing his eyes shut and shaking his head as if he is hurting.

Words bubble up from his lips: Portobello, Soho, Lola, aah.

The spinnaker girl glances at the peeling girl and her breasts jelly up and down.

Again I recall the day on the river in London.

In a tearoom, afterwards, a gypsy woman hovers at our table. Mister, you are blessed, her voice quivers. You have beautiful boys. Spend a pound for a cursed soul. My father glances around, sees we are being stared at, and digs in his pocket. He finds 50 pence. She palms it, bows and goes.

Then my Coke float lands and I have to twist the glass and lick, twist and lick to catch the vanilla froth overflow.

Skin tilts the glass as he pours, in the way my father does, so the beer does not foam.

– In London, he tells me, they tilt the glass so you fill the pint to the brim with unfoamed lager. In Paris they skim off the head of foam. But in Berlin they pour beer so that it foams up. It takes seven minutes to pour a good beer in Germany and if they pour it faster you can send it back.

— Like corked wine?

— Just like corked wine, smiles Skin.

☞

As I pee into a bowl of blue balls, James Dean looks down at me. He wears a red jacket and dangles a cigarette from his lips.

I zip up and run a tap. I flick up my hair with wet fingers, check myself out in the mirror. I find a train ticket in my pocket and roll it into a cigarette. I reckon I look just like James Dean.

The door swings open and Skin comes in. He takes in the whole scene at a glance and smiles.

My cheeks burn because I am caught out and because he so casually unzips his fly in front of me, as if to say: Hey, we are all men. You, me and Jimmy Dee.

I look away as his jet of pee makes the blue balls do a popcorn dance.

☞

Cawing seagulls loop in the sky above the balcony, hoping we will chuck bread or chips for them to catch in their orange beaks dipped in black ink.

— My sister died when the Berg River came down in flood, Skin tells me. The canoe capsized. I made it ashore but the river took her. They reckon she would have bobbed up sometime and floated downriver to the crayfish and sharks at Saldanha.

— I'm sorry, I mumble.

I look out towards Robben Island to avoid his eyes.

— I find it hard to recall her face, he says as he sips his Castle. But my brother will not fade in time. There is a filmy echo of his face in my Coca-Cola glass. I do not see him in a mirror, for the dead shy away from being caged in a mirror. My brother visits me in reflections with broken edges.

– It may be hard for you to imagine this, Douglas, but the hurt dulls in time.

He rests a hand on my head. Robben Island goes all Dali on me as I blink back tears.

⁓

The washerman waits shirtless in the evening breeze for his two rand.

– Go well, chief, says the washerman, bowing his head.

Skin does not appear to hear. He spits into his handkerchief to wipe away a smear of birdshit.

The washerman winks at me as we go.

We ride the coastal road through Clifton and Camps Bay, where in bygone days my mother and father would picnic in the moonlight under the palms. By the time we climb Chapman's Peak the sky is stained black and the lights of Hout Bay below are yellow seeds scattered by the gods. You can smell the sweet mountain fynbos. We curve ever higher into the night sky. The horizon is a deep orange, as if a fire burns out there where dolphins whine like dreaming dogs.

⁓

The feet of a sandpiper flit across my forehead. The feeling is so beautiful I dare not peek and end the magic. So I float on, blindly, craving another feathery touch on my skin. The hood of the Peugeot is still down and the sea wind gooses my skin.

I hear the whistle of a train. My eyelids part. Skin's face hovers over me, silhouetted by the moon. Daunted by my peeled eyes, his fingers flutter away. The train halts at Muizenberg station, just above the deserted parking lot, where we sit side by side in the Peugeot under the moon.

It saddens me, his fingers fumbling for his cigarettes in the cubbyhole. I want his fingers to comb through my hair, the way my father's did, but he is tapping a box of Texan cigarettes to pop one up.

An old man drops down from the train onto doddery feet. Then a posse of rowdy boys jumps out. They shadow the old man.

– Hey oupa, off to the disco? they taunt.

He says something about having fought in the war and they caw raucously. He shuffles across the tracks, shaking his head. The boys swing down towards us. The Rolling Stones warp out of a boombox radio.

One of the boys, his jeans slit in gaping gashes below his ass, picks up a Coca-Cola can and chucks it at a woman in a yellow bikini on a palm-fringed, billboard beach. Black tears of Coca-Cola run down her breasts and stomach. When the tears reach her bikini bottom the boy licks them away. The others howl like dogs at the moon.

The boys go down to the sand and crack open cans of beer from a backpack. Laughter and jigsaw words carry over Jagger's jaggedy voice and the hiss of the surf:

       tits

            shark

Tutu

       Yoko Ono

              cunt

– Your eyes are a beautiful blue, Skin whispers into his hands, cupped to light a Texan.

For a moment I wonder if I heard it. But the sentence lies among the jigsaw words and Stones lyrics, almost as physical as the box of Texans he flicks onto the dashboard.

He tilts his head up to drag deep on the cigarette, but does not look at me. His eyes focus on the rearview mirror before resting his hand on my hip. It is the same instinctive glance to the back seat my father always gave before his hand went to my mother's lap. I know I ought to feel dirtied, but I feel numb. This is the beach my brother died on and it is as distant to me as the billboard beach.

I wish I had not opened my eyes, then maybe the boombox boys would not have come and Skin would not have said the words that cannot be unsaid.

– I want to go home, I tell him.

He nods and turns the key. The Peugeot motor purrs under the bonnet. As we pull away, a voice hurls the words: fucking homos, at us. The others hoot with laughter.

– Bloody country, Skin swears through clenched teeth.

For a while he is silent. I watch his cheek bone rippling under taut skin. As we steer into Lagoon Road, he turns to me.

– I'm sorry our evening ended so sordidly.

I am not sure if he means the taunting of the boombox boys or his touching me. The Peugeot glides to a standstill under the coral tree and putters out. The front room flares up and I see my mother at the window, beyond the frangipani flowering white in the moonlight. Skin jumps out to open my door, as if I am a girl. He shakes my hand, ruffles my hair and flashes a smile at my mother. He is Gatsby, all charm.

– See you tomorrow, he calls as he skips around to his side.

He reaches for the dial and jazz fizzes up to the moon.

voodoo

Bessie Malan next door has a glass eye. It is blue. An ostrich pecked her eye out up in Oudtshoorn. The ostrich thought the eye was a gemstone, or a button. When an ostrich goes for you, the thing to do, my father used to tell Marsden and me, is wave a thorn branch at it. Bessie did not have time to wave a thorn branch.

Bessie Malan's white hair is a tangled crow's nest of fishing gut. Her glass eye she puts on a pine stump in the yard to keep an eye on the gardenboy, Matches.

At dusk Bessie Malan comes out with an enamel mug of coffee for Matches and pops the eye back in.

— Yo yo yo, says Matches, as he jives out the gate. He has traded his gumboots for the black-and-white alcapones he wears to joll around town.

A hoopoe has his digs in the dead pine stump.

— Tannie Malan, aren't you scared the hoopoe will fly away with your eye in its beak? I ask, as Matches's alcapones tap a jiggedy beat down the tar, glad to escape the mad madam and her voodoo eye.

— Blitz never hits the same bliksem twice, says Bessie Malan, sucking in her lips.

Her teeth lurk somewhere in the murk of her house. I wonder if she ever goes out with all her parts in.

Hope says the marble-eyed widow smokes dagga for the pain in her crooked bones. I am not sure, as I have never heard of whites smoking it. But the way Hope tells it, dagga grows like pumpkins in the Transkei. She says you can smell the sweet tang of it in the townships, through the biting stink of gum burning in steel drums.

One night Bessie Malan jumped from the footbridge into the lagoon and sunk to the beer-bottled sand. A vagabond abandoned a bicycle festooned with his belongings to dive in and save her.

Hope reckons her head was so stoked with dagga she thought she could fly.

– I don't want you filling the boy's head with stories of dagga and skollies, my mother scolds Hope, stabbing at a canvas with her paintbrush the way she stabs the jammed lid of a jar of jam to pop the trapped air.

My mother does not look up as I go out. I walk along the lagoon and cross the footbridge Bessie Malan flew from. A bony bird flapping featherless wings. Fishing-gut hair floating on the tide.

In Beach Road I cross at the zebra by the public pool. I stand at the railings, looking down on the pool. Beside me is a black man with his boy up on his shoulders. I recall my dad holding me up to see the banjos and umbrellas in the Coon Carnival of clowned lips and pink umbrellas and music oozing sweetwine sunshine.

I wonder what the black man tells his boy, who is forbidden by law to swim in this water.

– Ishushu namhlanje, the man says to me, mopping his brow.

– Ewe, ishushu, I nod.

Then I see Marta by the pool in a bikini and my heart goes rikkitikkitavi.

I fish out the screwed-up rand note to pay the woman at the gate to the pool. She folds it out flat with long fingers, as if handling a dirty handkerchief.

On the Kalk Bay harbour wall, as Marsden's ashes sink, Oom Jan slips a ten rand note into my hand, as if it is my birthday. My mother holds my other hand, and beside her stands my father, head bent down towards the water where gulls dive to taste the floating orange and yellow nasturtium flowers.

She holds Oom Jan's note up to the sun for the watermark, then she glares at me, as if to say: I know you young men and your tricks. Pool and cinema women are always bitter and wary. They would be doubly wary when Marsden and I stood side by side, as if our mirrored looks were a joke we wanted to play on them.

Marta lies on her stomach on a sarong on the grass by the side of the pool. Her watermelon-motif bikini is unhooked for tanning. Her ginger hair has escaped the pink rubber bands and spills over the border of her sun-faded sarong onto the grass. A wire runs from a radio to her ear. I can just pick up the bass.

– Hi, Marta.

But my voice does not reach through the music. I am not sure if I should touch her. I stand so my shadow falls over her face. Sensing that the sun is gone, her eyelids peel back and she squints green eyes at me. Her fingers hook up her bikini. I glimpse a sliver of untanned breast. One hand turns the radio down and the other finds her shades.

She rolls over, with the shades hiding her green eyes and the watermelon motif taut over her small breasts.

– Hi, Marta.

– Hi, she says, tentatively.

– It's me. Douglas. Remember, from the train.

– Oh ya. Howzit?

– Fine.

She shifts up to make space for me on her sarong. I sit on the edge, almost touching her skin.

She rattles a box of Beechies gum at me and I finger one out and chew it. The orange flavour fills my mouth.

I look up to see the black man and his son, still at the railings. I hope he will not see me, but he does, and waves. I wave back, feebly.

– You know I once saw you on the beach, says Marta. I was running with Shadow, my dog. You were walking on the beach with your surfboard. You had undone the leash and it dragged in the sand behind you. Shadow went after it as if it was a rat. He got it in his teeth and ran and jerked the board out of your hands.

She laughs.

– I think it was my brother.

– Oh. Sorry. I heard about your brother.

My eyes lasso a seagull, follow it till it fades in the haze. Then I study Marta's pierced earlobes. My mother says it is cheap girls who pierce their ears. My mother still wears clip-on earrings. She says the Hindus in Durban may run hooks through their skin, but she will not scar the temple of God.

– How does it feel, to be alone? Having been a twin.

I gaze up at a hang-glider surfing the sky.

– I'm sorry, whispers Marta. You don't have to tell.

I shrug.

– I still feel as if I am a twin. I still feel as if he sees me, as if he knows my thoughts.

– That's so mystical, says Marta.

There is a lull between us, as I have not thought of it as mystical, and I want to think it out for a moment. But my eyes focus on her earlobes again. It looks like a fish hook in the skin.

– Did it hurt?

– For a few days. You have to rub rum on the ring and keep twiddling it.

I do not tell her my mother would think she is cheap.

– Do you like it?

– I think it's cool.

But it is a lie because it reminds me of a time I got a fish hook in my finger so deep it hooked in the bone. It is the finger that is the barrel if you mimic shooting a gun, and your thumb is the cock. The doctor had to cut it out with a blade. Glancing at the arrowhead scar I feel a sick lilt in my stomach.

– Grazie, she says.

– How come you know Italian?

– My father is Italian.

– Italian is such a musical language.

This is something I have heard my mother say. She loves Fellini films. I grasp for Italian words but only *pizza* comes to mind. Then I remember *gelato*.

– A word like *gelato*. You could say it over and over again just for the sound of it. But there's no music in *ice-cream*. Maybe you could teach me Italian?

– Okay. *Zanzara* is mosquito.

– *Zanzara*?

– Good. And a *piovanello* is sandpiper, and *farfalla* is butterfly.

I wish I could stay forever, the damp from her bikini seeping into my shorts and the orange Beechie in my mouth and *zanzara* and other exotic sounds in my head.

– Your hair is so blond from surfing, she says.

The truth is, I rub lemon juice into my long hair so that it fades faster in the sun.

– Your hair is beautiful, I say.

I touch her frizzy ginger hair and she tips up her shades and stares her green eyes at me. I want to kiss the bare patch between her eyebrows, but the chittering girls from the train flock up to us and snatch Marta's green eyes away from mine.

I walk home barefoot along the tar. A fluke high tide has sent salt water over the sandbank into the lagoon. A dead seagull floats on the water and fish worry it.

Zanzara zanzara zanzara zanzara zanzara

My bare feet hopscotch along, dodging the cracks in the paving as Marsden and I used to do, long ago, when we still believed in manhole bears.

hip
hop
skip and
froghop
springbok
kangaroo
didjeridu

My name is Douglas. I am alive, though part of me, the me in Marsden, is docked. In one pocket I carry my father's Zippo and pocket knife. In the other pocket small change mixes with orange coral seeds. Perhaps it is true of the seeds, that they bring good luck.

I fall asleep whispering Marta's name into my pillow.
Green fish drift through swaying orange seagrass.

My head flies off the pillow. My heart pounds. My mind ferrets after the sound that woke me, frantic to catch it, defuse its horror by defining it, naming it. But all hint of the sound is gone, skoon out of my head. All I hear is the familiar ragged volley of Chaka's blunt barks, listlessly echoed by the other dogs of the neighbourhood.

The floorboards, cool under my bare feet, creak like a yacht mast in the wind. The zebra skin on the wall brushes against my skin. My mother stirs on the orange sofa in the front room. From the lip of a tipped glass, wine seeps into the floorboards. A candle on the window sill has burnt to a stub, oozing wax over the edge. The incense joss has gone out long ago, leaving a trail of fish-shit ash. Yet the smell of jasmine lingers, a wistful afterthought.

The kitchen door swings in the breeze, the moon glints off the lino. I sense that the sound came from out there, beyond the kitchen steps where Hope often sits and peels sweet potatoes into her apron at dusk.

teaboxes

I walk down the road from Valsbaai station to the Zandvlei lagoon, the path Marsden and I always walked home from school. Two Thomas boys eeny-meeny-miny-moed. Mo cast like bread to the fish, leaving me to foot a flat Coca-Cola can alone along the tar. Alone, unchased, unhassled by my shadow brother.

The clatter and clank of the can skimming the tar calls the bitter old monkeynut widow to her window.

She eyes me, chews monkey nuts and spits the shells into the winnowing wind. Though I am hardly in the mood, I can tell she is waiting for me to play my part in the old ritual. I pick up a stone to chuck at the red postbox on the corner.

– Joo got no respect for the neighbourhood, she yells.

Her banshee yelling would kill us, Marsden and me. We would giggle all the way down to the lagoon.

Muizenberg is full of old widows and the ghosts of faded men, their suits still hanging in mothball cupboards like shed snakeskins. After Dodi died in the Tote, my Nana was a mothball widow for half a year until she withered away.

– She pined for Dodi like a widowed lovebird, my mother said.

The window widow's eyes follow me, longing for me to

pick up another stone, but, as I am alone, there is no fun in it.

For me, the world has become a slow, dull turning under the sun. My father's typewriter gathers dust. Marsden's room is a museum of unfingered things, of warping ricepaper and cracking waterpaints. My mother treks deep into her painted landscapes. Marta belongs to the parakeet girls, tossing glances like small change to my poorbox eyes.

Down by the lagoon, on the footbridge Bessie Malan leapt from, a lone man handlines in baggy dungarees and straw hat. He is a character out of *Huck Finn*, fishing the Mississippi. He yanks the handline and a tiddly fish flinks against the blue sky. It flops onto the bridge, at my feet. The man stands on its tail and goes down on his knees to free the hook. His toes peep out of split tackies. He flicks the unhooked fish into a blood-smeared Jiffy bag full of shuddering, sardiney fish, too small to debone. He stands and wipes his hands on his dungarees.

– Yello, my basie, he says to me, tipping his raggedy straw hat.

– Hello. I haven't seen you here before.

– I'm here and there, my basie. I have been in the Roeland Hotel for a time. I tell you, life is sweet as hanepoot when you come out of jail.

I feel a jab of shame that I have been blind to the sweetness of life since the ball hit Marsden, hard as a flying halfbrick. The sun pelts down out of a blue sky. Just one wink from Marta spins my head. To cheer me up, Hope cooks butternut and bobotie and sweet potatoes. In the end, my mother always comes back to me from the places she journeys to.

The man picks up a cigarette stub and pockets it for the quarter inch of unsmoked tobacco.

– Lady Luck is smiling on me. I feel it in my bones. You haven't got work for me, my basie?

– I'm sorry.

– So goes it, he laughs.

A hoity-toity lady comes tiptapping over the bridge. The fisherman gives her space, and she tucks her handbag tight under her arm. I wonder if she smells the Roeland Street jail in him, or if it is a tic of hers that all coloureds trigger.

The fisherman mimics her hoity-toity walk, and I laugh.

– Hey, maybe you can fetch me something to eat. A koek, or a semmij.

– I can get you a sandwich.

At home, Hope is crying on the kitchen doorstep. There's nothing you can do when she cries, you just have to let her cry it out. I'll have to make the sandwich myself. I fling the fridge door open and go for the Danish ham. I doubt they eat Danish ham in Roeland Street. I cut two thick slices of Springbok bread and smear them with butter. I slice through the ham, and my thumb. The knife is so sharp, I don't realise I've cut myself until I see a drop of blood on the bread. I suck my thumb and it begins to sting.

I wonder, as I suck the blood from my thumb, if he escaped from jail, or if they let him go. On Radio Good Hope you hear of escaped prisoners hiding out on the mountain, but surely they wouldn't go fishing in the lagoon for all the world to see.

My mother's head appears over an Indian teabox. My heart sinks. Boxes mean change. Even dogs know that.

– Dee, I can't stay in Muizenberg any longer. This house is too full of morbid memories.

– I don't want to go.

– Dee, your grandfather's money is running out. I've found a cheap place in the Karoo, in a town called Klipdorp. Bessie will rent out the house and keep an eye on things here.

I imagine Bessie Malan's glass eye on the yard wall under the coral tree, keeping an eye on things. Perhaps the old coloured man will come along and pocket it and leave no eye to watch over the shadows of the dead and the exiled.

– I'm staying, I mutter.

– Bayview will be happy to have the books we don't want.

She chucks Homer's *Odyssey* onto a pile of musty hardbacks.

I hardly know my mother as she shifts boxes and piles up books. If I told her I wanted to pierce my ear, I doubt she would flinch.

Hope is sniffling on the doorstep.

– Ulungile? You okay?

My words unleash a howl from her. I give up and walk back to the bridge to give the fisherman his ham-and-blood sandwich.

For me the Karoo is another world: foreign, far, flat and bleak. No surfing, no Marta, no lagoon.

He smells the sandwich.

– Ham. Hey ay ay. I tol' you Lady Luck is smiling on me.

dog's eye view

My father has gone, beyond Seal Island, beyond the horizon. Now the rest of us trek out, away, from. My mother is behind the wheel. Hope rides shotgun beside her. I am in the back with Chaka.

My mother steers left into the Strandfontein road in my father's old Benz, Indlovu. She drags under the loaded roof rack and the full boot. The orange corduroy sofa is to follow us by rail.

Chaka juts his head out the window to bite at the wind, and slobber hangs from his jowls like frogspawn.

Hope reckons she is glad to escape the Langa skollies before they fill her windpipe with Omo and, besides, Peddie is not as far by bus.

My mother's face is a mask but I know she is churned up inside, as the gears catch with a cry of steel teeth as she goes into third.

Hope's chickens kick up a racket on the roof, caged behind my grandpa's crocodileskin suitcase so their feathers are not plucked by the wind. Chaka barks madly, the gears grind and Hope cries *ayeee ayeee ayeee* because she will miss the Cape, even if skollies run free.

We drive past Sunrise Beach. There is a hard sea running

ashore. The beach is clotted with seagulls in the sand. They sense a storm is coming.

Vygies flower on the dunes and root the dunes down in the wind. Cows stray over the dunes into the road. Their eyes are wide with wonder as a dog's head yelps by.

Bye-bye dunes, beach, sea. Bye-bye brother. Will you still visit me in the Karoo, or will it be a place devoid of shadows and reflections? Bye-bye Marta. I wonder, would you have let me kiss you if the parakeet girls had not come?

We cross over the N2 and see coloured men walk along the roadside, bent under jerrycans of Friday sweet wine.

Thunder rolls and rain begins to fall hard. Zigzags fire the sky over the Simonsberg. Two avocadoboys huddle under a flipped-over wheelbarrow, like a twin-headed tortoise. A Xhosa mother with her child tied to her back stands under a stone pine, risking the skyfire to keep her bundled child dry. Chaka hides down behind Hope's seat and whines in fear of rumbling gods.

As we drive through Stellenbosch the rain dries up and the light is an unearthly green. The water sloots of Dorp Street overflow and the road is a shallow river. A Camel carton floats by my window, chasing akkerdoppies.

I wish we were coming to live in Stellenbosch, rather than crossing the mountains into the desert. From here you can still catch a ride down to the Strand to surf after school in the afternoon, but once you go over the Simonsberg and down through Pniel into Groot Drakenstein, it is another country.

In the coloured town of Pniel we pull up at a petrol pump to fill up for the long trek ahead.

In a Pniel café, I ask the coloured tannie, the café auntie, for a can of Coca-Cola, please ma'am. She throws in a banana for free, for the English boy.

I switch to Afrikaans:

– Dankie, tannie, vir die piesang.

Coloured girls titter at me from the shadows where dried boerewors hangs among bananas, a rainbow of hairclips, cheap tartan-handled pocket knives and long bars of blue soap. An Indian mynah caws at me and the girls titter again when I hop away from the cage.

Back in Indlovu, I tell my mother.

– It's sweet, but rather unusual, for a white boy to call a coloured woman auntie, my mother reveals.

Groot Drakenstein: fruitpickers are blurred specks of colour in the rows of vines. My mother turns up the dirt road to Oom Jan's farm to tell them we are trekking out to the boondocks.

There used to be whispers in Cape Town that it was moonshine that made Auntie Tia, my mother's sister, give up the fizzing life of theatre and cafés she had in Cape Town for a dull life in the Boland with a boer.

Once, driving back to Muizenberg over the mountain, when the folks thought Marsden and I were dozing in the back, I heard my mother remark to my father: I wonder how such a bull of a man makes love to a woman. My father laughed, and said: Maybe you dream of it? Through squinted eyes I saw his hand snake past the gearknob towards her lap. My mother giggled. My father glanced in the rearview mirror and caught me peeking. His hand jumped to the dashboard to fiddle with the radio dials and *Year of the Cat* leapt out of the radio.

It is a pity we will just stay for tea, as Oom Jan makes his own boerewors, stuffing the mix of cow and fat and spice in long gut skins, flimsy as the rubbers you sometimes find on Sunrise Beach at dawn. The spices for his boerewors are a secret, like the recipe for Coca-Cola or Kentucky Fried Chicken.

I love Kentucky. Sometimes on Friday evenings in Muizenberg, we would pick up a keg of Kentucky and go to the drive-in.

My father hides Marsden and me in Indlovu's boot, to smuggle us in to see One Flew over the Cuckoo's Nest, *since we are too young for the 2–18 film. I love the feeling of lying coiled up against my brother in the boot. Twins, breathing in the same dust and dog smell, and hearing my father's beers rattling.*

Auntie Tia and Oom Jan come out to meet us, while Dirkie hangs back sheepishly. The dogs jump up against Indlovu at the sight of Chaka, pawing at the window, barking at their old friend and at the chickens on the roof. Oom Jan boots the big boerbull bastard dog in the ribs and the boerbull's yelps mix with Chaka's frenzied barks, and the *yip yip yip* of the fox-hunting Jack Russell hanging on the boerbull's heels, like a pilotfish shadowing a shark. I jerk back the handle and Chaka catapults out. The dogs cavort and caper around Indlovu, so that Hope is too scared to get out.

– Voetsak, Oom Jan yells at the dogs, and they bound away into the vineyards to bark at guineafowl and rabbits.

I imagine Chaka telling the boerbull and the Jack Russell stories of chasing seagulls on Sunrise Beach, and the farm dogs thinking: sassy sea dog.

– Bloody dogs, grunts Oom Jan.

He gives my mother a kiss as she steps out of the car.

– It is good to see you, Sarah. But I hope you are not going to go through with this Karoo trek of yours.

– Jannie, leave her be, says Auntie Tia.

She gives me a sloppy kiss on the mouth. Her mouth is always syrupy, as if she has just had a slurp of hanepoot. As soon as she goes around to hug my mother, I wipe my mouth dry. Then I remember Dirkie, and look up to see him watching me.

– Kom nou, jong, Oom Jan calls Dirkie.

Dirkie shuffles over.

– Hello, Tannie Sarah, he says.

– Hello, Dirkie. Don't I get a kiss?

My mother bends her head so he can kiss her. Hope, seeing that the coast is clear, climbs out of the car. I can tell Oom Jan finds it odd that Hope should sit in the front. I imagine him thinking: Typical Capetonians. Full of liberal ideas: driving around with chickens on the roof and a hoity-toity hotnot up front.

Hope goes around to the back of the house, where she can drink tea from enamel mugs with their maid, Meisie.

We sit on the stoep, and Meisie appears with the tea tray of china cups and scones and gooseberry jam. Dirkie gazes out over the vineyards towards Paarl mountain, as if he has never seen the view before. You would think I was the dead twin. Oom Jan digs around in his pipe, and then taps the old tobacco into a potted oleander.

– I wish you wouldn't do that, chides Auntie Tia.

– Tia made the jam herself, you know, chirps Oom Jan.

He is keen for us to see how his wife has adapted to farm life, giving up fancy things like bridge and the theatre for things that you can hold, like jars of jam and bricks of butter. Somehow, it comes out as an accusation of women like my mother who buy their jam and butter at Spar.

– Sarah, stay with us on the farm, says Oom Jan. The boy can go to school in Paarl with Dirkie.

Although Oom Jan knows that it is Marsden who is dead, and therefore Douglas in front of his eyes, it is an old habit of his to sweep away any doubt whether it is Marsden or Douglas by calling us *boy*.

– And me? Shall I be your concubine? my mother mutters, as if commenting on the view.

Oom Jan spits a mouthful of tea back into the teacup. Auntie Tia lifts her teacup to hide a smile. Dirkie is puzzled. I do not think they learn much English in Paarl. I am not keen to go to Paarl after all Dirkie's stories of the headmaster, Ou Langhans, who canes you if your blazer is unbuttoned, or if your hair tickles your ears, or if your shoes do not shine.

– No, really, says Oom Jan. It is not right for a woman to go gallivanting around the bundu with a paintbrush. These are violent times, you know. You could end up with a panga in your head.

– Jannie, for God's sake, Auntie Tia pleads.

After tea, we bundle back into Indlovu. Chaka's panting mists up the windows.

– Totsiens, Meisie calls out to Hope.

Under my feet is a box of Merlot wine from the farm. I wipe the mist from the back window so I can see them wave at us. Oom Jan has his arm around Auntie Tia, and she looks like a reed beside a rock. His other hand is on Dirkie's head. His hand says: I am your father and you are my son. This is your land and your destiny.

On the outskirts of Paarl we veer towards the mountain and climb the winding Du Toitskloof pass. Below us lies a patchwork of vineyards and orchards, and dams glinting in the sun. We swing around a corner and the road is full of baboons.

My mother keeps her foot light on the pedal as she weaves Indlovu through, so the baboons do not jump on the roof and rip the chickens out of their cage.

I have to wind up Chaka's window. Kamikaze fool dog thinks

he can take on a whole tribe of baboons. His barks chisel into my head.

Hope reaches for something to throw at the baboons. Whenever she sees a snake or rat or any wild thing she instinctively stones it. She does not care if it is a tobaccoroller or molesnake or any undeadly animal. There are no stones in the cubbyhole, so she flings a shot spool of Kodak film at the baboons.

My mother swerves to the roadside as there may be photos of Marsden on the film a baboon is sniffing. She hoots the horn to scatter the baboons, then reverses up to the cast spool.

– Dee, you go for the film while I hold Chaka.

I gear myself for a shark-fanged baboon to dart from under Indlovu and jaw my hand. But I pick up the spool unscathed. I swing the door to. Chaka licks my ear as the grunting baboons home in again. My heart drums and I feel faint as we drive on up the winding road. I shall miss my father being around for when things get scary, like the time Marsden and I found a mamba in the yard.

Hope is all for stoning the snake and Byron wants to spike it with a pitchfork, but my father calmly lures it into a wine box and folds in the flaps. I have the box in my lap as we ride Indlovu out along the Strandfontein road to free it in the dunes.

My father would pick up in his bare hands the vleifrogs Marsden and I found in gumboots in the garage. He would catch spiders in jam jars and throw them out into the night. Like dark thoughts, the furtive furry things would find their way back after a few days. I wished he would kill them, as I never got used to the spurt of fear on discovering a spider in my cupboard.

Everything goes black as we are sucked into the mouth of a tunnel. The dark bears down and squeezes out any sea breeze still lingering in my lungs.

As we come out into the sun and drop down into the Hex River Valley my lungs fill with still, dry air. There are no fan-blades in the sky. The sun is a white eye. It sees all, like the glass eye of Bessie Malan.

Chaka's slobber dries out and he pants bergwind gasps across my face. He gazes out over a landscape of stones to the edge of your sight, and dogs see far.

⌒

The dorps on the N1 go: Matjiesfontein, Vleifontein, Leeu-Gamka.

We head through a land of bald koppies and karakul sheep for a town called Klipdorp, in the far Cape, south of the Orange Free State border. Other than the picnic bays in the sketchy shade of bluegums every few miles, there is no shade.

A hawk drops out the sky to the parched earth. Then it flies up to a telegraph pole and tugs a string of lizard gut away from a flicking tail.

The road follows the telegraph poles, an unending echo of totems.

On long journeys, when Marsden and I were small, we would begin to fight like tomcats in a basket. My father would call out: First one to spot a lion gets ten cents.

We would sit still for miles and miles, eyes skinned for the telltale twitch of a tail among the Smartie-coloured cosmos. We never saw a lion, but my father would sometimes fork out five cents for an ostrich or a donkey.

At Beaufort West we turn off the N1 and stop at a BP.

– Fill up with 97, says my mother to the black petroljockey in a grasshopper-green overall.

He hooks in the pipe and Chaka goes bananas again. I feel

ashamed that we have a racist dog. He loves Hope and Byron, but all other blacks are postmen or newspaperboys to bark at madly.

The petroljockey comes round to my mother's window.

– Check oil and water, Madam? he says calmly, as if he is used to whitefolk dogs and their drooling fangs.

He twists open the radiator with a handkerchief from his pocket. He jumps back as rusty water fountains into the sky. Indlovu gurgles and hisses unhappily. The man fetches a can of cold water and Indlovu glugs a canful.

– I could shoot the bloody dog, my mother snaps.

We head for the N1 again, Chaka still barking his head off. My mother is so rattled by his barking that a big rig almost runs us down just as she steers onto the highway. The rig swings to avoid us. Indlovu screeches. The rig horn wails and it feels as if we will be sucked into the slipstream. There is a stink of burnt rubber.

Hope cries, my mother's face is bleached and Chaka is dazed.

Behind us the petroljockey flicks his tip into the air and catches it in his hip pocket and I think of Bessie Malan's eye in a deep tobacco-flecked pocket.

Chaka dozes off in my lap. My mother, regaining colour after the rig scare, tells the history of Klipdorp as we go along.

– Klipdorp is called Klipdorp because there is no river or mountain or kloof that landmarks it, just a pyramid of stones a pioneer digger from Amsterdam unearthed in his bid to find gold there.

Chaka farts as his legs jerk in his dreams of scattering baboons, or of catching seagulls that taunt him from the sky.

– Later they found out that, by some fluke, the digger's pyramid was halfway between Cape Town and Johannesburg. Over the years caravans of drifters and fortune-seekers camped on the riverless flat, halfway between the fruit and the gold. So it became a dorp, Klipdorp. Then, one day, an old diviner's fork danced in his hands. But the Klipdorpers laughed at him because any old fool could tell the earth under their feet was as dry as death. They doggedly oxed water all the way from the Zeekoe River for the rest of their lives.

Hope shakes her head at all this whitefolk history.

– It was only after the Boer War, when the boers came back to farm, after years of warring against the English on horseback, that a drill was sunk into the rock and sweet water flowed to heal the land.

My mother chose Klipdorp because of an advert in the paper for a house going cheap in the charming, undiscovered Karoo. Before my brother died, my mother would study the ins and outs of everything beforehand. We never went on holiday without her reading all the guidebooks she could find in the second-hand bookshops in Long Street. Now she buys a house she has never seen, in the middle of nowhere. To hell and gone, as Oom Jan would say. All she wants to do is paint, and Muizenberg does not inspire her.

– Muizenberg is too European, she says. The Karoo is rugged and that's what I want.

So, just because my mother wants ruggedness, we head deeper and deeper into the outback. I do not see the charm of this landscape of stone and dust and thorn.

⌒

After miles and miles of karakul sheep: Klipdorp. The digger's pile of stones is long gone. No river or mountain to mark it, just a sign saying: WELKOM IN KLIPDORP. It is the kind of white boondock town you drive through, dipping down to 60 for a few kays. You may stop if petrol is running low, or if the engine is smoking, or if you need to pee. Then you kick up to 120 again, following the tar through the bald veld, maybe catching a glimpse of the black shanty township a few miles beyond the dorp, out of cozy white eyesight.

Delarey Straat, the main road, runs as the crow flies through the dozy dorp.

Wind-pumped water fountains like liquid cacti on the front-yard grass. Fences blur as morning glory and granadilla wind through the wire.

Rhodes Hotel: a deep Victorian veranda and a gnarled, ele-phantskin oak, dropping acorns into the dry sloot.

Dutch Reformed kerk: the tall spire spears a blue sky. A bird flies from the spire, handlining a shadow along the tar.

A jail with barbed wire on the walls.

A bottlestore with big adverts for Castle and Black Label and Klipdrift. A man kips on the kerb in front of the bottlestore, his head under a floppy hat.

There is a thatched Anglican church with stone walls. It looks as if a giant dug up a sod of England and dropped it in the Karoo. The priest is in the graveyard, hosing the cannas, tongues of red and orange flame like the flames that danced on heads at Pentecost. The graveyard is not a restful place to lie, as now and then, randomly, a motorcar or lorry hurtles by.

Then the town peters out into desert again and Indlovu U-turns and heads back through town. This time I see the black man sitting on an upturned beer crate at the Shell, across the road from the Rhodes Hotel. He has the white seafroth beard of an old man and a teacup patch of bald skin on his head. He catches me staring at him and waves his yellow handkerchief at me. By the time I wave back we are quite far down the street and I am not sure he sees my hand wave, like the nodding head of a felt back-window dog.

We pull in at the Sonskyn Kafee to get cool drinks and ask for the way to 9 Mimosa Road.

Coloured kids play hopscotch on the paving outside the café. A girl with her hair in long stiff pippielangkous plaits hopscotches from square to square and, flamingoing on one skinny leg, reaches for the stone, while the other kids clap their hands.

There is nowhere to sit outside. It is not that kind of café.

By the door, firewood is bundled with strips of bicycle tube, same as you use to make a cattie to kill starlings. Strings of wine-gum beads hang in the door to keep the flies out.

At first it is hard to focus in the dark, but then I make out the café tannie with her hair tied up in a bun. Above her head are the cigarettes: Texan, Camel, Lucky Strike, Marlboro. Behind her are coffees: Koffiehuis, Van Riebeeck and Frisco. And the teas: Five Roses and Joko. On the counter are the newspapers, and Lion matches, and sweets: Chappie's, niggerballs, Kojak lollipops. The shebang of colours and flavours, just as you find it in the Sea Breeze Café in Muizenberg.

It feels good to find such familiar things in a foreign place.

From the rattling fridge I grab a Coca-Cola for me and a Canada Dry for Hope. My mother does not drink fizz. She reckons it just makes you thirstier. She drinks gallons of tea early in the morning and stores up the liquid like a camel until her first gin and tonic in the evening. Indian tonic is bitter, but my mother enjoys bitter and spicy tastes, dry red wine that makes your tongue tingle, and mango atchar that stings your lips and burns your ass afterwards.

My mother buys firewood, a newspaper and Springbok bread.

– The house is not egzekly on the corner. There is a rugby

field on the corner, and the house is by there, the café tannie tells us, her lardy white arm signposting the way, somewhere beyond the pinging pinball machine.

The braai meat we find next door in the Karoo Slaghuis. The butcher's apron, dark blue with white kudu stripes, is smeared with blood.

Butcher: Karoo lamb is juicier –

Saw: *vuzzzz*

A chop, bread-slice thick, drops from the teeth of the saw onto newspaper.

Butcher: and sweeter –

Saw: *vuzzzz*

Butcher: and cheaper –

Saw: *vuzzzz*

Butcher: than down in Cape Town.

Saw: *vuzzzz*

The butcher plops the newspapered chops and a coil of boerewors on the counter and wipes his hands on his apron. Under the glass of the counter, meat spiced a vivid orange is threaded on sticks like Hawaiian flowers.

Overhead a fly, lured to a pink bar of light, dies in a spit of flame.

Butcher: Enjoy it.

At the Kommaweer bottlestore, my mother runs in for a sixpack of Castle dumpies.

– Too hot to drink red wine, she chirps cheerfully to Hope and me as she hops into Indlovu again.

9 Mimosa Road: the walls a dirty white, red paint peeling on

the wavy zinc roof. A dry bougainvillaea forms a canopy over the stoep. The house looks bare after our house in Muizenberg, where hibiscus and frangipani and Pride of India hid it from the street. A lone, thirsty jacaranda casts sketchy shade in the yard. The house has an abandoned, cursed air to it. No wonder it is cheap.

A gaunt, raggedy-feathered bird perches on the roof. Chaka barks at the bird and it flaps away in gangly flight.

VERKOOP slants red across the TE KOOP sign. A Mevrou van Zyl from next door comes over with the keys and a melktert she has baked for us.

– It is a change to have folk from Cape Town come to us. Usually folk work their fingers to the bone in the hope of a place by the sea one day, she says, shaking her head.

– Yes, it is beautiful by the sea, my mother smiles sweetly.

Then why on earth are we in this far-flung, voetsak dorp? I wonder.

– Ou Willem, God rest his soul, dreamed of dying there by the sea in Onrus with his mouth full of geelbek fish.

The buffalo grass sends out snaky runners across the yard in the hope of finding water. The skull of a kudu bull is nailed to the stoep wall.

– Ja-nee. He had to do with tinned sardines, she laughs.

I sense it is a joke she has told before. I hear mice, or rats, skitter away through the tangle of bougainvillaea. Black ants drip down from the skull. So, some things survive.

Our neighbour on the other side from Mevrou van Zyl is the rugby field on the corner. Though it is midsummer, boys are playing rugby. The buffalo grass under their feet fades to cowskin patches of dust. Chaka pees against the fence to mark his turf and then races up and down the fence to bark at the boys.

The barefoot boys stop their playing for a moment to stare

at the stranger and his crazy dog, but then they play on, ignoring Chaka and me. The boys are lithe and sinewy. There is something jaunty and cocksure in the way they drop a shoulder before spinning out a pass. The flick of a hand to glide the ball. I sense in the stirred-up dust of impala feet that the boys are born of the earth.

Though they know I am there they do not call out to me. In a way, I am glad because I have never had an instinct for the zigzag bounce of a rugby ball. Just as I have never foreseen which way life will tack. It is all random to me. A fluke ball kills Marsden. A blind corner throws up a band of baboons. A whim casts us into exile in the desert.

A shiver ripples through me because the Klipdorp boys look so hard and because fate is so haphazard. There are six coral seeds in my pocket and I finger them as if counting out an over in cricket.

⌒

I see the bird is back on the roof. I reckon it is a buzzard, or a vulture of some kind. I throw a stone at it and the bird jerks into flight again as the stone clatters on the zinc.

– What on earth? calls my mother, jutting her head out of a window.

– It was a buzzard. Or a vulture, I lamely mutter.

– Oh for God's sake, Douglas, leave the poor bird alone.

My mother's head is gone again. One moment she wants to shoot Chaka for barking, then she feels pity for a buzzardy bird.

I turn to mend a hole in the fence so that Chaka does not run out. From across the street, a barefoot, tanned girl watches me. Sun flames her tangling, gypsy hair, casting her face in shadow. Sunlight filters through the cloth of her dress, revealing the inside of her legs like a secret.

I abandon the wiring. I want to do something eye-catching to hold her gaze. I pick up a dry jacaranda pod that looks like the hard shell of a river crab. It has a good weight in my hand and would be good for skimming and skipping over water.

Sunflared deep resin pool in the Berg River. The trout stay down in the shadows. Dirkie, Marsden and I, we know they are there and we flick the fly hooks in and out to tease them out. Flisk flisk, the fly whisks past my ear. But the fish stay in hiding. We drop the fly rods for flat stones to skip over the river. Dirkie is the skipper king with fourteen hops.

I toss the pod for Chaka to chase. He catches it in his teeth as it falls, claws up dust on the turn and jikas his head as if gulleting a rabbit. I imagine the girl awed by my cold-blooded dog. But when I look again the barefoot girl is gone. I feel marooned.

Tossing a jacaranda pod to hook a girl. You bloody fool.

His stub ablur, Chaka chews the pod at my feet. Dumb cur. I feel an urge to hurt him, to hear him yelp for being so blind to my feelings.

I kneel to drink from the raintank tap. The water is sour.

I find a ladder in the garage and climb to the top of the tank and peer over the rim to see if something has fallen in to sour it.

A mangy dog-hide floats in a reflected sky. The reek floods my head and I feel dizzy. The ladder sways. The tank pitches away from me and the sun races across the sky. I am Icarus falling into the sea. It will be cool and deep.

But there is no sea under me and the earth is as hard as clay fired in a kiln. I am dead, until I feel Chaka's slobber on my face.

Hope thinks death has swooped down on us again and cries out to God:

– Tixo Tixo Tixo.

My mother comes running out, drops to her knees and scoops my head up in her lap.

I feel the lilt of the dog-water in my stomach and want to be sick. The earth tilts again and I cling to my mother.

– There is a dead dog in the tank, I tell her.

– Yo yo yo, Madam, whines Hope. This is bad magic.

– This is no juju, says my mother, just local boys trying to scare us away.

She combs her fingers through the long strands of my lemon-juiced hair. I recall my father's lifeless hand on my head at dusk on the rocks and begin to cry because there is no father to chase jinxes away, or to bury dead dogs. My mother holds my head to her breasts, as she did on Christmas day. Over her head I see the buzzard land on the roof again.

☞

When the water runs dry I tie a handkerchief, bandit-style, over my nose and mouth to dull the stink. I climb the ladder again to fish the rotting dog out with a wire hook. Now that I get a good look at it, I see that it is not a dog, but a jackal.

Long Beach. Marsden and I are five. We find a dead duiker in the dunes with maggoty eyeballs and crabs scuttling to hide in the gaping stomach. One brave crab creeps out, pincers up. We pee on it.

I dig by the fence, watched by the beady-eyed buzzard. The jackal lies dead in the sun, and flies buzz around. Chaka, usually full of bravado, hides on the stoep. He smells that the jackal is a wild thing.

The earth is too hard by the fence and I give up and dig where the tankwater has drained. The spade sinks deeper this time. I dig fast and then use the spade to shovel the jackal towards the hole. The spade cuts into his pelt, and blood and water ooze out of a gill slit. I vomit on the grass. My head reels and I use my hands now to drop the jackal in the shallow hole. I claw sand in with my fingers.

Then I climb down into the rain tank to scrub it free of scum.

Oom Jan's farm. Dirkie and I squeeze through a hole in a big steel wine vat to scrub it out for pocket money. Marsden is too scared and we taunt him, calling him moffie, moffie, our voices warping, echoing in the vat.

I wonder, as I scrub, if stranded seagulls and buzzards and drowned jackals are signs that death and misfortune have not stayed in Muizenberg under the eye of Bessie Malan, but followed us here, riding the roof with Hope's caged, scruffy chickens.

The kitchen window sill is a clutter of teas: not the Joko or Five Roses you find in shops but Darjeeling and Red Zinger and Ceylon. Teas sent by my mother's friends from around the world, the parcels torn and taped up again by the customs men to check it is not dagga or something evil from overseas.

My mother brews some rooibos tea to still my stomach. I carry the smoking mug through echoing rooms to my bare bedroom with the window to the rugby field. Until the orange corduroy sofa arrives by rail, I am to sleep on the floor. My books tumble from the crocodileskin suitcase I inherited from Grandpa Thomas. I can still make out his ports of call, stamped in black ink: Cairo, Zanzibar, Lourenço Marques, Durban, Cape Town.

I stack the books against the wall in a corner:

The Old Man and the Sea, with the old school stamp and a seagull feather in it.

Cry, the Beloved Country, hiding the postcard I stole from my father's drawer of a mermaid with bare breasts. I wonder how the photographer got her skin to blend into fish scales under her bellybutton. I imagine Marta naked, her tangling red hair coiling down like wisteria to hide the nipples of her budding breasts. I hide the mermaid inside the slow sad book again, feeling guilty I have harboured so sinful an image when Marsden is dead.

To Kill a Mockingbird. A fishmoth falls from the binding. I smudge it dead under my finger.

Of Mice and Men. Though I have read it half a dozen times, I still cry when Candy's blind and stinking dog is shot.

My father's fingered copy of *The Outsider.* I open it at random and read the note pencilled in the margin: *In the eyes of M. all experience is equal. Whether he stays in Africa or goes to Europe is irrelevant. One existence is as good as another.* I wonder if it is irrelevant for Miss Forster whether she is in Cape Town or in Amsterdam. Somehow I feel sorry for her living in a cold, flat city. I feel a longing for her, like a longing for KitKat when you have been surfing for hours.

I spark my father's Zippo and picture him docked off the east coast of Africa, sipping a lonely whiskey, dreaming of me, Dee, longboard boy.

Dark glides in through the window and dams in the room. I sit alone in the dark, surrounded by the dark. Outside, the sky is still blue, tinged with pink. There is a scratching sound. I think there are rats in the roof. Then quiet again. Then I hear the humming of telegraph wires plucked by a dusk wind.

Against the black screen of my drooping eyelids I see my father and Marsden and me at sea on the Hobie Cat. My father's hand rests on the tiller and the sun is in his hair. He is carefree and Marsden and I hike out, our backs skimming the water. The sail is drumskin taut. Then he lets the sail out an inch and the Hobie keels, dipping Marsden and me under a wave. It is a game he loves to play.

⌒

I zippo the *Cape Times* from the unpacked Indian teaboxes, and the pyramid of firewood catches. It is the first time I have ever braaied, because my father always used to braai. I turn the coil of boerewors all the time to make sure it does not burn. I feel like a man, with the tongs in one hand and a beer in the other.

Hope is to eat with us, although she usually eats alone in her khaya off her yellow enamel dish that she keeps under the kitchen sink. My mother gives her a china plate. You can tell it is a big thing for Hope to eat off china, as she keeps brushing her skirt with one hand, flattening her spongy hair with the other.

We all drink Castle out of the bottle, something my mother used to say was uncivilised. The world has turned on its head and I feel giddy as I stare into the firelit amber of the beer.

I listen for the soothing radio static of the sea and the zither of mosquitoes. Instead there is the zing of crickets and the call of an owl. Somewhere in the distance, there is a volley of gunshots. A farmer shooting at a jackal or a stray dog. A policeman shooting at a stonethrower.

I imagine the barefoot girl alone in the zinging, Karoo night, spinning on a koppie under the scattered stars.

Inside, the house is empty of memory. Outside, frenzied moths dive at the street lamp.

It is good to feel the seeds of the coral tree in my pocket.

counting crows

The school is in Palm Straat, a palmless street of trimmed flower-beds, scarecrow gnomes and birdhouse postboxes. There is a brick wall around the schoolyard that makes it look like a jailyard. Although Klipdorp is just a dorp, boys and girls come to school from the farms round about and board in the hostels. I am called a dayboy. I am free to go out of the school walls during break, when the boarders have their tea and sandwich in the hostels.

An unscared crow perches on the wall, catching torn corners of sandwich flipped to him by clowning kids. *Kaah kaah kaah,* goes the crow.

Counting crows: *one for sorrow, two for joy, three for girls and four for boys.*

When the bell goes, the crow flaps off. The boys and girls jostle into rows, to be marched to the hall. Because I stand apart, a teacher snaps at me. So I fall in, and follow gleaming black shoes into the hall, a PT gym. There are no chairs, just rungs to climb the walls and ropes hanging from the roof, so we sit cross-legged on the floorboards. The looped ropes remind me of hangings in cowboy films.

When the headmaster, Meneer van Doorn, comes in, we stand. His black hair is slicked into combed rows to hide his baldness. His cheeks are hollow and his skin sallow. He scowls for the fidgeting to end.

– Good morning, school. You may be seated.

We all sit.

– Will Douglas Thomas stand.

I stand up again, so all the shaven-headed boys and green-skirted girls can see me, the boy from Cape Town, from another planet.

– This is Douglas, from Cape Town. It is his first day in Klipdorp High. I trust you will help Douglas find his feet, says Meneer van Doorn.

They nod, as if to say: Oh yessiree.

Three for girls. The girls in green skirts just stare at me, curious to see a boy with the flickaway hair of a surfer.

Four for boys. Fear darts down my spine as I sense the hatred towards me from shaven heads.

Meneer van Doorn's voice rambles on, but I do not catch his words, as a boy spits the word *moffie* in my ear and jabs me in the ribs. I gasp with pain. Cape Town candyass, whispers another. I feel a pang of bitterness towards my mother for landing me in this backveld dorp where the boys and girls smell the sea in me the way wild birds smell the tameness in freed cagebirds.

My first lesson is biology, with Meneer de Beer. He is a tall man with tortoise-shell glasses that warp his eyes, like the melting clock in the jettisoned Dali print.

The others have come to the class with lizards in jam jars.

Some of the lizards have lost their tails. I have never been in a class with girls or lizards before.

Under Meneer de Beer's Dali eyes, the lizards are slit open to study the way they tick. The girls flinch, but the boys stick compasses into the quivering lizards.

The slitting of the lizards reminds me of a story Miss Forster read to us, of how two old aunts pluck the feathers out of a bird because it spied on them. Then they poke its eyes out. Then they cut up the bird with a knife. I remember the sound the finch makes as it is plucked, it pipes. But the lizards in Meneer de Beer's class spill their insides soundlessly.

When the bell goes for break, I go to my locker to fetch my sandwich. The locker is wired shut, because I do not yet have a padlock. I unwind the wire, and take out my tuckbox. Hope has made Black Cat peanut-butter sandwiches for me. She knows I hate the way peanut butter clings to the roof of my mouth, and has made up for it by mixing it with honey. My favourite sandwich is cold Kentucky on bread, but there is no chance of that in this dorp, where there is no Wimpy, never mind Kentucky.

I leave my school books in the locker and wire it up again.

Though I am free to go home, I choose to stay in the schoolyard in the hope of finding a friend. I sit against the wall. Around me is a chaos of squabbling and clowning. I bite into my Black Cat peanut butter and honey sandwich and my teeth find something rubbery. I peel the sandwich apart to discover a dead lizard in the peanut butter. I feel dizzy and my skin is clammy with cold sweat.

I sit on the flagstones, staring at the lizard. There is a blurred scurry in the corner of my eyes. I look up to see boys closing in on me like fielders closing in on the last batsman. I look for a gap, but there is no escape. The boys drag me behind the bicycle shed. At the command of a lanky boy they call Joost, they yank down my shorts and underpants and bundle me into a wicker basket the size of a wine barrel.

– Carry him to the main road, barks Joost.

Through the weave of the basket, I see him walking ahead. He is the white hunter, his porters stumble after him.

I am the prey, carted down Palm Straat, then along Delarey. They drop me at the foot of the Boer War obelisk in front of the town hall, where a stub-footed beggar begs on the steps.

– Okay, boys, run, commands Joost.

I hear their laughter ebb as they run away. The beggar edges towards me, but before he reaches me a stray dog comes up to the basket and sniffs at it.

– Go away, dog, I plead.

He ignores me and cocks his leg to pee.

– Voetsak, hond, I yell in Afrikaans.

This time he bolts, and the beggar backpedals.

Dog pee drips through the weave onto my head. This has gone too far. I flick up the lid of the basket to see an old tannie peering quizzically down at me. She prods her walking cane at me as if I am a tiger wanting to escape. The cane digs into my ribs and I pluck the lid down and dog pee rains down on me.

– Shame for you, she cries out.

A jamboree of onlookers gathers and the bitter old tannie beats the basket with her cane. Eyes bore through the weave and the beggar unwinds a wire hanger, as if to jemmy open the door of a motorcar, and feeds it through the weave. Rather than be kebabbed on a wire, I will chance the stares and jeers. I lift the lid again. The cane swings down on my head and the beggar giggles. I want to run but my legs feel lame.

Then I see Hope in the crowd. She stands there, laden with Spar bags, eyes wide as cow eyes.

– Au au au, Douglas.

My words are all ajumble. I am no tiger from the jungle. Just a scared boy with lemon-juiced, dogpee hair. Hope pulls the doek off her head to cover my dangling thing. I sense they find it distasteful, her doek on my white-skin snake. As if it is cocky of her. She puts her arm around me. We cross the street, my ass bare as a Kalahari bushman's. The wolf whistles make me want to scoot.

– Walk with your head up, says Hope.

We turn the corner by the Post Office and I skedaddle.

Halfway across the rugby field by our house, I step on a devil thorn. I hop on one foot while I pinch it out of my heel. It burns like hell. I hop along lopsidedly, my songololo ajiggle. As I reach the fence dividing the rugby field from our yard, the fence I wired up to keep Chaka in, I see the barefoot girl with the gypsy hair on a bicycle.

‿

She, barefoot girl, now in black sandals and white socks, reads on a bench in the schoolyard in the shade of a plane tree. Some of the seeds have fallen and split under soles, spilling a film of fluff on the stone paving. There is a circus of skipping and tagging and jostling going on around her. But she is still, as if the shade of the plane anchors her.

I stand and stare at her. Her eyes jerk away from the book because a horsefly or something stings her calf. Through the laughter and babble I hear the smack of her hand on her skin. She spits in her hand and rubs it in. I wish I was close enough to see the speck of blood. Instinctively I look around for a Muizenberg lollyboy on a bicycle. Ice is good to take the sting away, but there

are no lollyboys on bicycles in Klipdorp. Before I can think of
another plan, she is lost inside her book again.

I walk past her, fingering the seeds in my pocket. I whistle and
swivel my head as if the schoolyard is full of exotic things: fla-
mingos and macaws, instead of bricked-in kids. As I reach her, I
chance looking down. Her head is bent. She wears rubber bands
in her hair like Marta, not pink but green to match her school
gym. The hem of her gym has been let out. It is a bottle green
while the rest of her skirt is faded to olive green. Between the lip
of her skirt and the book is a shadowed gap. The book is bird-
winged in the wedge of her knees. It has the red blur of a library
stamp on the edges. I catch the title from the top of the page she
is on: *Born Free.*

And then I am past her, my heart drumming and my head
giddy. I look back at her and know she is in Kenya, running with
lions on the beach sand, lions old man Santiago dreams of, coun-
tries away from me and the other kids in the school. I wish I could
follow her there and run with her and the lions, the sun flaring in
her gypsy hair and the Indian Ocean salt on her skin.

In my mind, she runs in Marta's watermelon bikini. Or in
green panties. In the short time I have been at Klipdorp school
I have discovered that girls have to wear green panties to match
their uniform. Green hairbands, green gyms, green panties and
no lipstick or mascara. Boys may wear underpants of any colour
because they zip up, but girl's skirts flip up in the wind like
Marilyn's.

Another thing I have discovered is her name. Marika. Magic.

The bell goes and I have Meneer Bester for PT. He played
rugby for Natal in his time and has a skew, flat nose. Nowadays he
spends the summer by the pool with his shades on. He chucks a

waterpolo ball into the pool, then parks off in his deck chair. Now and then, he randomly blows his whistle, maybe so the classroom teachers will think he has a hard job.

☙

In the water I am as fluid as the rugby boys are on land. Like a penguin, so swift in the waves after an ungainly plod across the sand. But this only deepens their mistrust of me. They do not pass the ball to me and I end up swimming alone under water, coming up for air at the wall and sinking again to swim another length under water. As I glide, my stomach skims the tiles and I yearn to stay down forever, cool, enveloped, time-warped.

The platanna frog is clever. He knows we are going to shoot him when he comes up, so he stays down till we give up. Dirkie reckons a platanna slows his breathing down, or breathes through his skin.

Under the water, skimming the tiles, I feel as if I can breathe through my skin.

I come up to find the pool deserted. Meneer Bester's deck chair flaps in a gust of wind. I am late for Meneer de Wet's class and I am suddenly scared, as my father is not there to chase fear away. He has sailed to Malindi, or maybe Mombasa, and may still sail beyond the horizon of memory.

Marsden, my frogkiller brother, steals back among the black pines of the past.

☙

Meneer de Wet has a hooked nose and darting eyes. He reminds me of the buzzard on the roof.

– You're the new boy in town, he says, but I cannot turn a blind eye to such disregard for time.

He bids me to bend over his desk. My hands rest on piles of unmarked essays. Two cuts. Just a friendly reminder.

To keep from crying I reel off all the sea fish I can think of: hottentot geelbek kabeljou galjoen snoek dassie zebra zeb

shotdown birds

I sit on the veranda of the Rhodes Hotel with my mother. The floor is waxed a deep red, as if stained by ox blood. My mother sips her gin and tonic and fans herself with the menu. The skin under my knees sticks to the pink plastic chairs and I feel beads of sweat run down my calf into my sandals. My mother frowns at me when I slurp up the last of my Coca-Cola through the straw. My slurping is the sound of a cappuccino-mixer in a café. I finger out the block of ice and put it in my mouth. If I were alone I would bite the ice, another thing my mother hates. I just let it melt in my cheek.

Across the street is the Shell Garage. The black man who waved the yellow handkerchief at me the day we came to Klipdorp is there, sitting on the same upturned beer crate. His eyes pan as cars go by, as if he is watching a game of tennis. The afternoon sun slants down on his white hair and he mops his forehead with the handkerchief. There is no shade under the canopy that juts out over the pumps from the garage building. I imagine it is still hot enough for the petrol to flame without a match.

A Ford bakkie pulls in, with four black men standing on the

back. The petroljockey jumps up, pockets his handkerchief in the
ass pocket of his faded red overall. He is nimble for an old man.
The name sewn in yellow on the back of the overall is *Jim*. He
touches his forehead to greet the white driver, who is alone up
front in the cab. Then he goes around the back of the bakkie to
unreel the petrol hose. There is upbeat banter as Jim fills in the
petrol. I catch the Xhosa word: *ewe.*

The black men are all in the blue overalls of farmboys, but the
youngest of them has unbuttoned the top of his overall and tied
the sleeves around his hips. I see the grooves of his hard, wash-
board stomach. The young man does a gumboot jig on the back
and the others all laugh at his jaunty antics. The white man bangs
the window, and waves his fist at the young man, as if to say: Don't
you get too cocky, boy.

The young man bows his head, turns away, then widens his
eyes in mock fear for the others to see. They kill themselves again.
The white farmer, sensing he is the butt of the joke, climbs out of
the bakkie and stands there on the bulky legs of a rugby prop, his
veldskoens apart. He wears one of those khaki cowboy hats with
a fake leopardskin band around the brim. The laughter dies, like
shotdown birds. I can just make out the black of a comb, stick-
ing out of his long socks like a scorpion wanting to crawl out of
a crack. My father always said to me: You can tell an Afrikaner a
mile away by the comb in his socks.

The bulky farmer swings his fist at the young man, who tugs
his head out of range like a boxer. The farmer loses his footing
for a moment and his leopardskin hat falls to the tar. The farmboys avert their faces in shame. Jim picks up the hat and dusts it
off with his handkerchief. The farmer snatches his hat out of Jim's
hands. I feel awkward witnessing this with my mother beside me.
It is the squirmy feeling I get during a sexy scene in a film when

my mother is watching with me, that I am partly to blame for what is happening on screen.

– Men can be such bastards, my mother says.

I had thought it was a certain kind of man who was cruel, but my mother's words make me feel there is something in all men that is shameful.

Then the farmer digs out his wallet, curved from sitting on it in the bakkie all day long. He licks his fingers before counting out the rands. Jim fingers the buttons of his hipbag, like the buttons of a trumpet, to give the man change. There is no tip for Jim. The farmer taps a pipe against the sole of his boot, so the dead tobacco drops out. Then he bites the pipe and climbs back inside the bakkie. The diesel motor catches and throbs deep.

The farmboys wave to Jim as they go. He gets an old Castrol tin and uses cardboard as a brush to sweep the tobacco into the tin. He empties the tin into a bin with a swinging lid, and then settles on his beer crate again.

The ice in my mouth is now melted enough to swallow it.

– Do you think you'll be happy here? I ask my mother.

I am thinking of her painting, and whether she will find the inspiration. She puts down her gin and tonic and sighs:

– Dee, I can never be happy again. Perhaps there will be moments of happiness, but there will always be the pain.

I too feel the undertow of pain tugging at my feet, drawing me down to shadowy, kelpy depths.

– Aren't you at all happy now, with me?

– I love being with you, Dee. But you'd have to be blindfolded not to see how cruel life can be.

I chew my straw to stop myself crying. I will never be enough to make my mother happy.

My mother turns to history, perhaps to cheer me up.

– You know there was a time when Delarey Straat, in front of us, was called Victoria Street. After the Second World War, when Malan came to power, the Afrikaners changed the names of streets to honour their boer heroes. This was their way of mocking the English who killed their women and children in the camps, and tried to kill their language.

Lulled by the lilt of my mother's voice, my mind drifts to the sea. I look down from a seagull's view of the tidal pool at St James. Beyond the lagoon calm of the water, the Atlantic crashes against the breakwater.

Standing on the breakwater at dawn, our backs to the vast blue of False Bay, Marsden and I wait for the big wave. I see a shark finning through the still water of the tidal pool. I shout: shaaaaark. But it is too late. The wave breaks. I drop to my stomach. The wall is as sandpapery as coral under my skin.

Then the wave is over and I jump up to call out to Marsden, who is in the foamy pool. Beyond him is the shark. Marsden sees the fin and freestyles like crazy towards me. The shark zones in on the wounded-fish sound of his kicking. I catch Marsden's hand and yank him out. The shark veers away, skimming the wall. I look into his cold, cat eye, before another wave breaks and we drop to the wall again. When the foam clears, we see the fin at the shallow end, as if the shark surfed the wave in. We run along the wall to shore before another wave breaks.

Three coloured men come walking along the beach and we point out the shark. One man runs over the rocks and comes back with an old tennis net. Two of them unroll the net and drag it across the pool, from the deep end in, sweeping the shark to the shallows. Though there is a gap under the net the shark feels trapped. Then the third man wades in and clubs the shark on the head with a long wooden oar. The shark tosses his head towards him and he skips aside, lithe as the mongoosey snoekseller dodging motorcars. He clubs it again and skips away again, until the shark sinks.

They drag the shark ashore by the tail, slit his white stomach to spill his guts. Some they toss to cawing seagulls but the rest they bury in the sand for stray dogs to dig up. They tie the shark to the long oar and two of them hoist the oar onto their shoulders. The third man, the clubber, rolls up the tennis net as if he has just played a set or two. They wave totsiens to Marsden and me.

Then we cycle home for breakfast, picking up fresh Portuguese rolls and the Cape Times *at the Sea Breeze Café for breakfast. My father reckons it happens sometimes, by a fluke of the tide, that a shark is washed in, but they are usually sandsharks and their teeth are too far back to take a bite out of you.*

– And one day, perhaps, Delarey Straat will be called Mandela Street, or Tambo Street. So you see how history is in flux.

The history teacher at Klipdorp High, Meneer Jansen, has this way of killing history stone dead. He makes us underline key words and dates in our history textbooks and number the facts:

1. <u>Jan van Riebeeck</u> arrived at the <u>Cape</u> in <u>1652</u>.
2. He <u>bartered cows</u> for beads from <u>Harry the Hottentot</u>.
3. He gave the <u>free burghers</u> the right to farm the land that came to be called <u>Stellenbosch.</u>
4. In <u>1688</u> the <u>French Huguenots</u> fled the Roman Catholics in France and settled in <u>Franschhoek</u> to plant grapes.

And so it goes. He has taught out of the same textbooks for so many years, and the facts have been underlined so many times, the pencil often goes through the paper when you underline again. If you hold a page up to the sun the light shines through like a Chinese lantern. It does not help to point this out to Meneer Jansen.

We underline the facts again, to imprint them on our minds.

– Let me tell you, fingerwags Meneer Jansen, history is not like biology where you poke holes in lizards. One lizard more or less is neither here nor there. Twenty-six thousand boer women and children died in English camps during the War. Ja-nee, history is not made up of cold numbers like maths, where you can rub out mistakes. No, in history we do not rub out or poke about; we remember.

As I sip another Coca-Cola I run through the facts in my head for a test on the reasons for the Groot Trek. The Dutch farmers did not want to give up their slaves. They did not want to learn English and give up Dutch. They did not want to bow to an English god.

Thoughts of the Dutch go west as I become aware of the waiter at my elbow. He is an old coloured man called Ou Piet Olifant. He says he comes from District Six, the part of town at the foot of Table Mountain that the government bulldozed down. Ou Piet Olifant remembers the banjos and mandolins and the sugar girls and groovy-time bars. He has nowhere to go back to. The world of his youth is gone like it was just a bioscope flick.

While Ou Piet Olifant conjures up the ghosts of District Six for us, he fans his face with a plaid cloth cap. It reminds me of a pub in England.

An old man fans his cloth cap over a smoking bowl of mulligatawny to cool it. Then he cups the bowl in his hands and drinks from it like the French drink coffee at breakfast. Under the table he has slipped bootless feet under a black-and-white sheepdog. My mother tells Marsden and me not to stare. When I drink the pea soup from the bowl I get a clip on the head from my father.

– It is a crying shame, says my mother, about the death of District Six.

– It's a mystery, nods Ou Piet Olifant. I mos fought in the war agenz Rommel's tanks, but when the poleez came we jus' stood there and watched the bulldozers ride our place flat.

My hamburger is cold. It looks like a pat of cowdung, so I drown it in ketchup. My mother frowns at the farting sounds the ketchup makes. She has a Greek salad with Calamata olives and feta and quartered tomatoes.

I wonder if the Cape slaves who were hanged, drawn and quartered were dead while being drawn and quartered. I would like to ask my mother, but I sense she is already queasy at the sight of all the ketchup bleeding from my hamburger.

bad magic

I pedal listlessly down Delarey. The sun beats down on my head and stings my scalp. I turn in at the Shell for a cool-drink from the icebox. Jim jumps up from the Carling Black Label beer crate.

— I see you, young baas.

— I see you.

— What is your name, young baas?

— Douglas.

— Douglas. A strong name.

He makes me smile, but senses my sadness.

— Kunjani? How are you, young baas?

— Ndilungile, I say. Alright.

I am not floating (I cry for Marsden and my father and my Muizenberg teacher-mother) and I am not sinking (for I long to see the sun filter through Marika's skirt again). I am just barely lungile.

— Oh. You speak Xhosa?

— A few words. Ndifuna Coca-Cola, Mister Jim.

— A good day for Coca-Cola. But, my name, young baas Douglas, is Moses, not Mister Jim.

– Then why is *Jim* sewn on your back?

– I will tell you my story, young baas Douglas, but first the Coca-Cola.

He bends his head into the icebox for a Coca-Cola and I see his lagoon of bald skin. He digs a can out and taps it three times with his finger before handing it to me. I finger up the ring pull and it fizzes cheerfully. I feel it is rude not to offer him a sip, but then I have never drunk from the same can, or cup, as a black man. I think of Hope's yellow enamel dish, under the sink so it does not hobnob with the china. I feel his eyes on me.

– You drink, young baas, he says, as if he senses my doubts.

– Sure you don't want a sip?

– No no. You have been to school, reading and writing big things.

I shrug and drink a deep long gulp.

– Me? What have I done, just sit on my box and watch the cars go by.

He laughs a deep laugh that rumbles up from somewhere in his drumskin stomach. It spooks the mossies on the overhead telegraph wire. They flit up into the blue, and then flutter down again.

He reaches into his deep overall pockets and scatters seed for the mossies. They fly down to peck at the seed. Then, a black crow drops out of the sky and caws at the mossies until they abandon the seeds for the telegraph wire. Moses flicks his handkerchief at the crow to shoo it away, but it just darts a beady eye at him and dips down for the seeds. The mossies twitter on the wire. There is something slick and rat-like about the bird. It is like a seagull hungry for fish heads, but lacking all the cheeky charm seagulls have.

Moses wildly flaps his arms to chase the bird away, then settles on his empty beer crate again.

– I tell you my story, young baas, says Moses.

He reaches deep into his pockets to pull out an orange packet of Boxer tobacco.

– I am a Xhosa, from the Transkei. I spent my days as a man down the mines of Johannesburg. One day they said: you are too old to dig for gold. They put money in the post office for me, and said: Go home to the Transkei. But in the Transkei, there is nothing for me. My mother and father are long dead. I have no wife, no children. So I thought to myself, all your life you heard stories of Cape Town, of the fruit and the fish and the flowers. So now is the time to go. I was on my way down to Cape Town on this N1 road when I got a lift from Beaufort West on the back of a farmer's lorry carrying sheep to the slaughterhouse. Twelve miles north of Klipdorp, the farmer picked up more sheep and there was no room for me on the back. The seat up front was free but he did not offer it to me.

Moses tips the Boxer tobacco into a furrow of squared newspaper.

– So I walked down the road under the burning sun, the jacket of my father folded over my arm. Then two white boys in a bakkie went past. The bakkie turned around and I knew there was going to be trouble for me.

He licks the edges of the newspaper.

– I had to jump out of the way of the hooting bakkie. When it went past I heard the words: Ride him dead. The bakkie turned again, kicking up stones. This time a boy put out his hand for the jacket I carried. The dogtooth jacket an English soldier gave my father long ago in the white man's war. The jacket with my pass and the moneybook in my pocket. Gone.

In my mind, the bakkie roars off, leaving Moses flapping his hands, as if chasing crows, or drowning in the dust.

Moses lights the cigarette with a Lion match.

– When I got to Klipdorp I saw a boer leaning against the diesel pump. I said: Baas, let me drink from the tap. He said: Go ahead. So I drank and ran cold water over my head. He said: Hey, old man, there's a drought in the Karoo, don't you know? I tipped my hat to say *ndiyabonga* and began to walk away. He called after me: Hey, old man, you want a job? My petrolboy Jim just landed in the jail.

He glances down Delarey towards the Klipdorp jail.

– They found out this petroljockey Jim was ANC. He was jailed in the jail down the road, but then they took him to Pretoria. There has been no word of him.

He shakes his head.

– So, my post office book was gone and I had no imali. It would be a good thing to have imali in my pocket for Cape Town, I thought, so I said: Yes, baas. Just for a time.

Moses handkerchiefs the beads of sweat from his forehead.

He bends his head, and the tobacco smoke hovers over his bald head.

My father's trick: he breathes cigar smoke into a glass of Jack Daniel's whiskey and, instead of billowing out over the lip of the glass, it hovers over the tiger's-eye liquid until it fades out.

The patch of bald skin and the crow's feet at the corners of his eyes are the only signs that Moses is an old man. He draws in a deep suck of tobacco, lifts his head, and goes on:

– I can go nowhere without my pass. The post office will not give me my money. They will not believe I am me, Moses, until I produce my pass. I wrote to Pretoria a long time ago, a year now. But still no pass comes in the post, and no word from Pretoria. For now, I am lucky the Klipdorp police do not trouble me. They do not check for my pass, for they know me, Jim the petrolboy. But if I go to another town and the police catch me with no pass they will put me in jail. I was jailed under the earth for too long. I am too old to be in a sunless place again. I think to myself: Moses, you are lucky to be in the sun, untroubled by the police. So I sit on my box and wait for my pass to come.

He laughs ruefully, flicks the cigarette to drop the ash.

– Young baas, people have called me Jim for two years now. So.

– I will call you Moses, if you call me Douglas, not young baas.

– You will make an old man happy. It is good muti for the old to hear their name in the mouth of the young.

He sucks deeply at his cigarette.

– Tell me, Douglas, why is there rain in your eyes?

– My twin brother is dead and my father gone.

– Gone?

– Sailed away.

– Yo yo yo, Douglas. This is too much bad magic for one boy.

For a long time we just sit under the black umbrella of bad magic, until Moses sweeps the gloom away.

– How old are you, Douglas?

– Fourteen. And a half.

– Fourteen. A big boy. Almost a man. You know, when I was a boy of fourteen, I still herded cows and goats in the Transkei, Umtata way. All day in the sun, down by the river, chasing wild dogs away, shooting birds, catching lizards. We herdboys fought with sticks as long as spears, not to hurt, but to learn the skill of a warrior.

Moses leaps to his feet, flings his empty hands overhead in a blurred flurry, as if parrying sticks. Then he shuffles to a stand-still. Sighs for lost youth. Takes a drag on his flaring cigarette.

– At night, when the coals died down and the tokoloshe walked under the moon, I lay down on the mat on the floor of anthill and cow dung. My heart beat against the bone of my mother's back. I breathed in her mother smell. Surely, in my mother's khaya, where my fingers combed through her hair, the tokoloshe would not dare? You know the tokoloshe, Douglas?

I nod, as Hope has told me vivid tales of the stumpy hobgoblin with the fiery red eyes.

– As a boy it was forgiven to cry, to curl up against your mother, to piss out of fear for the tokoloshe.

I laugh so hard the Coca-Cola fizzes out of my nostrils.

– Ewe. It is true. I pissed out of fear. But the longed-for time came when my father said I was to become a man. I was sixteen then, just two years older than you are now. I hardly knew my father, who was away on the mines all year. I too wanted to be a miner, to follow in my father's footsteps. To be a miner was to be strong and brave. My father told me it was hard down the mines, that he wanted his sons to follow another path. He said it was better to work on a farm in the Cape, for though you still left your wife and your children behind, you were outside, under the sky. To be under the earth was to die a slow death. But I did not believe him. I saw the men who came back from the mines, flashing money and shiny shoes.

Now that my father has sailed away, he is becoming a stranger to me. In my mind his face is fuzzing at the edges. His eyes are a deadpan, soulless stare. The glint is gone.

– To prove our manhood we had to do one daring deed. In the old times you would hunt a leopard or a lynx, but they were hard to find. So we chose to kill a dog that barked at us whenever our mothers sent us to buy bones or a pig head at the butcher. The butcher in our village was a bitter white man who lived in an old caravan. We hated that dog, the way he snarled and lunged at us, baring his teeth, fighting the rope that tied him to the caravan. One night I stalked up to the caravan when the dog was snoring and cut the rope. Then, from a distance, we whistled to wake the dog. When he ran to us, we speared the dog with sticks we had knifed at one end. It felt good to kill the dog. Years later, I saw that it was not the dog that was evil, but the man who taught the dog to hate.

The memory of it bends his white-fringed head and a sigh whispers from his lips. Then he lifts his head to suck long at the cigarette stompie. Wisps of smoke flow through his yellowy, cobby teeth as he goes on.

– My father and the fathers of my boyhood friends sent for the old tribal doctor, the ingcibi, to come with his assegai and make men of us. On the day the ingcibi came to our village, we boys of sixteen or seventeen smeared each other from head to foot in white ochre. Painted white, we would stay unseen by the evil spirits that waylay boys on the journey to manhood. For a moment I wanted to laugh at the sight of my black boyhood friends standing there white as ghosts, but I did not laugh, for I remembered the pain to come. The time for boyish fooling was over.

Moses stubs his cigarette out under his boot.

– We sat naked on our heels, the way bushmen do, waiting in a row for the ingcibi. We were surrounded by our fathers, and the other men. I wanted to catch my father's eye, but knew I was not to glance around like an inquisitive boy. I was to stare ahead, and go through with it. If my face pinched with pain, I would shame my father. The shame of being a coward would dog me forever. I would never walk among men with my head held high. I would never be a soldier or a miner. I would run away, my bleeding tail between my legs like a scared, stoned dog.

I glance down at the scar, recall the fish hook in my finger on the Kalk Bay harbour wall, recall my father's words: Be brave, Douglas. Cowboys don't cry.

– I heard the drums and I saw the ingcibi shuffle his scaly feet towards us, his spine bent, so his head was level with the earth, as the head of a tortoise is. Tixo, guide the hand of this old man, I prayed. Out of the corner of my eye I saw the ingcibi swing his assegai. Ithi uyindoda, he said. Say you are a man. I heard a young voice cry out: Ndiyindoda! I am a man!

I shudder at the thought of an assegai scything through my skin. Instinctively, I clasp at my songololo.

Moses sees me squirm. Laughs.

– For one crazy moment, I too wanted to save my cock. To run for it. But then I saw my father's unsmiling eyes on me. I wanted him to give me a sign that the pain to come would not be too bad, but his face was as cold as a mask. The ingcibi stood before me. I would not shame my father. He pinched my foreskin in his fingers, tugged at it and sliced through me in one swing. The burn flamed through my guts, my bones, my head. It was a pain way beyond the pain of a deep thorn or a dog bite. I saw the mouth of the ingcibi chewing unheard words. I saw, as if it was a leaf falling slowly slowly, my foreskin fall to the sand. I heard the cry of a man escape my mouth: Ndiyindoda! I saw my father's teeth smile. I picked up my foreskin and swallowed it before the evil spirits could get their hands on it and bewitch me.

I feel faint. I hold the cold can of Coca-Cola to my forehead to keep from keeling over.

– Afterwards the ingcibi wound a weed around my burning cock, bound it on with a leather thong. Then, we draped blankets over our heads, for no women should see us abakwetha during the time of change. For three months, my friends and I camped

out in the bundu, far from the village. It was winter, a good time
for healing. We made a grasshut shelter, a boma, where our cocks
would heal in the smoke of burning wet wood, where the men
came to visit, one by one, to teach us the things of a man: the history and traditions of the Xhosa, how to kill a man, if need be,
and how to sow your seed in a woman.

I turn my face to Delarey Straat, where oleanders flower pink
down on the island that splits the road. How will I learn to sow
my seed in a woman if I do not go into the bundu and I have no
father to teach me?

– At the end of the time in the bundu, we burnt down the
boma. The men of the tribe came to fetch us abakwetha, still covered in white ochre. We sang as we went, imagining how the girls
would eye us, how our younger brothers would skip at our heels.
Down at the river, below the village, we stood on the bank. My
father, his eyes smiling, undid the thong. At the sound of the drum,
we threw off our blankets and ran into the water. We ran to dodge
the gaze of the girls and the sticks of the men which bit at our
backsides. We ran to outfoot the evil spirits who try to catch you,
just before you reach the far side of this in-between world. In the
river we rubbed the clay away, laughing at how black we were after
months of being white. We came out of the water, fully men, no
longer boy-men, abakwetha. They rubbed red ochre on us, a sign
of our manhood, and gave us new blankets. We hugged the given
blankets to our shoulders, and walked tall up to the village. At the
place where the men gather, we were given our first beer to drink.
The beer had been brewed in deep pots by the women. As we sol-
emnly sipped at the sour beer, we saw our old blankets burn in a
bonfire, along with the things of our boyhood: oxen made out of
bone, wild animals out of wood or clay, our catapults and sticks.
Then the dance, the umgidi, began with the killing of a cow.

I think of the way my father let me sip the foam off his beer on the stoep on summer evenings in Muizenberg. Sometimes if he was deep in his newspaper, I would gulp down a mouthful of beer. The first time he gave Marsden and me a beer to hold in our hands and sip was when we watched the fireworks shot over the lagoon on bonfire night. Amstel beer. Originally from Amsterdam, where Miss Forster flaunts her flimsy frocks. We had turned fourteen just two days before. My mother said we were too young. My father said to her: when you were fourteen you went to a beach party in Clifton, on the back of a motorcycle. He pinched her behind and she swatted his hand away. Boys, he said to us, your mother was a frisky filly. You are lucky I lassoed her. Though I sipped it slowly, over hours as the fireworks flowered the sky, the beer made my head swoop, and the stars spiral. After the fireworks, Marsden and I jumped naked from the bridge, Bessie Malan's bridge, and fished dead fireworks out of the seaweedy lagoon.

– Douglas, I think this dying of your twin brother, the going away of your father, was the beginning of your bundu time, the time of your hardship. You are in the in-between world, when the spirits will try to catch you. It is a lonely, hurting time. But you will come out of it a man. Look at you. Though you bleed, you do not cry. A pity your father does not see you become a man.

blue reef

The English class. We are taught by a man called Mister McEwan. He is bitter about being stranded in this dull Karoo after teaching in England.

— In my school in England the buildings went back to the time of Shakespeare. Here in Klipdorp the oldest building is the jail, built as an English fort during the Boer War. This place is devoid of history or culture. I try to teach you Wordsworth and Blake, and your heads are full of boerewors and sheep dipping.

Joost yawns. It is a story they have all heard before.

— You know Tolkien was born in Bloemfontein. A monkey stole his clothes from the washing line. A tarantula bit his head.

Joost and the others pack out laughing.

— A baboon spider maybe, goes Joost. I never heard of a tarantula in Africa, sir. Maybe he was born in Brazil?

— Anyway, frowns Mister McEwan, after the monkey and the spider, his mother took him back to England.

— Moffie, jibes Joost.

— He never came back to this damned place, spits Mister McEwan.

I put up my hand.

– Why did you leave England, sir?

He looks confused for a moment. Giggles swirl around me. Perhaps he finds the question rude. I wish I had shut up.

– It's a long story. One thing led to another, he sighs.

He fumbles in his leather bag for his book.

– Now, open your poetry books to the poem by William Wordsworth.

He reads us a poem about daffodils, something you will never see in the Karoo.

– Daffodils are like cannas, only yellow instead of red or orange, Mister McEwan tells us.

I see the others stare out of the window. The world of dancing daffodils is too foreign for them. Marika, of the tangling gypsy hair, is reading a library book hidden behind her poetry book. Mister McEwan believes he has reached one soul in this barren land and glances her way whenever he draws in a breath. Marika scratches her knee and leaves those white lines you lick to make go away.

– Douglas, surely you have seen daffodils?

– Yes, sir.

Joost van der Berg wanks his fist at me.

Then Marika looks up from her book and smiles, at me, daffodilboy. A wonderful cappuccino feeling fans through my stomach. She turns back to her book, but I rewind her smile again and again in my mind.

The bell goes. As I walk out the class, Joost comes up to me, slings his arm around my shoulders.

– Hey, china, he tunes.

I wonder if maybe Joost is not biltong hard after all.

– I just want to warn you, McEwan fancies your melktert ass.

He winks at me and runs to catch up with his friends.

Not Joost or anything can pull me down, for Marika smiled at me.

I cycle to the Shell to tell Moses. He is filling up an orange Ford Capri with 93. I help him by wiping the windows. The woman inside is so fat the motorcar sags on her side. The suddy water warps her face. As I pass the window she catches my hand. The sour smell of her sweat wafts to me as she digs a finger in the dashboard ashtray. She flips my hand over and puts a coin in my palm. Fifty cents.

– You are a good boy, she says.

– Thank you, ma'am, I say, wishing she would let go my hand.

In the end, the Capri splutters to life and lurches lopsidedly away. I sniff the coin for sweat, but it smells of cigarette. I am glad to be alone with Moses.

– Moses. You know the girl, Marika? She smiled at me.

– Hey hey hey, Douglas. A good sign. And what did she say?

– She just smiled.

– Ah. No matter. She smiled. A good sign, he laughs. You know the time I came out of the bundu? After being painted in red ochre, there was the dance, the umgidi. All the village was there. My mother too. I was sad I would never sleep in her khaya again, but all the girls came to see us young lions and I could not dwell on my sadness. There was one girl with beads on her hips, and cheeky breasts. I longed for her to smile at me, but she stared down at her feet. I danced wildly, my sweat dripping like blood down my redclay skin. When the moon was high, and I wanted to drop to the sand, she looked at me and smiled. And then there was wildfire in my feet again.

I laugh.

— Just one smile and it makes you crazy. You know there was a time when a young man would lie with a girl, one who might become his wife, so she would wipe the red ochre off him with her skin. Sadly, I had the red ochre wiped off with fat and had to dream of the girl.

Moses pinches tobacco from an orange packet of Boxer tobacco and drops it into a furrow of newspaper.

— You know all my man years went down the mine, Blue Reef. Sounds beautiful, Blue Reef. But there is no beach down there: no sun, no sugarcane, no banana palms. Just black like death. The lamps on the hard hats burn like fire.

He rolls the newspaper and runs his tongue along the edge.

— As you drop down miles and miles in the cage, the sun is a far memory. You wonder if you dreamed your boyhood herding cows under the sun. You wonder if you dreamed the green hills, for when you come up out of the black, the sun goes down. There is a bus to the barbed-wire compound for Zulus and another bus to the barbed-wire compound for us Xhosas.

One end of the cigarette he twists, the other end has tobacco dangling from it.

— Through the window of the bus the land is flat and foreign. No mountains or rivers or cow kraals. Just black-and-white roads, and the far orange glow of Jo'burg over the mine dumps.

Flecks of tobacco fall from the cigarette. A mossie lands to peck at the tobacco, then flits away. Moses lights the dangly end. It flares, then dwindles to a glow. It fires orange again when Moses sucks in.

— In the Transkei, as a man, you smoke a pipe and drink sour homemade beer at dusk, the time when boys steer the cows home and children chase chickens and the women make a fire. In the

Transkei it is the magic time when voices carry across the valley and you can hear a dog bark miles away.

He sucks at the cigarette, and goes on while the smoke filters through his teeth:

– But in the compound at night the laughter of men who have escaped the black death another day is mixed with sad songs and the longing for women. When the revolution comes, the men joke as they rub away dirt with cold water: We gonna taxi to Hillbrow, drink Johnnie Walker on the rocks, see the girls shake their skinny white ass at us.

A gust of wind cartwheels a carton of Lucky Strikes down the street until a sackman spikes it. It reminds me of the way the skollies kill you in the township. Alleysharks hide bicycle spokes up their sleeves. You walk down an alley, whistling maybe, or just jingling the cents in your pocket. A spoke slides between your ribs like a blade through a watermelon. You may be tempted to laugh at the sudden blooming of a red rose on your shirt. So Hope tells it.

– My dream was not of whiskey and girls, but of Cape Town, sighs Moses. In my dream, I pick an orange, walk down to the sea and let cool water wash over my feet. I peel the skin, bite into the orange and the sweet juice fills my mouth. After a day in the night of the earth my Cape Town dream healed my dogtired bones.

The driver of a jam-packed taxi van calls out to Moses in Xhosa, all the while hooting at imaginary dogs. Without slowing down he twists his head around to keep Moses in sight, so the van runs blind. When the hub grazes the kerb, the driver swings his eltonjohn shades around to the road again. But just then a black girl goes by, swinging hips for all the world to see, and he twists his head to flick out a pink tongue through white teeth.

Cape Town. iKapa. Paradise. There is fruit and sand and sea, but the fruit farms lie inland. In Cape Town hawkers sell oranges by the sea, but the oranges come from Zebediela, up north. If you want to pick peaches or plums, Cape fruit, you have to dodge dogs and jump fences. It is even forbidden to pick up the fly-stung, windfall fruit. And, if you are black, you eat fruit on the tar kerb, as the beach sand lies beyond the signs that bark: Whites Only.

On the junkyard wall, jagged glass teeth glare in the sun like the cracked bottles on the walls of the Roeland Street jail in Cape Town. Roeland Street where, Oom Jan says, they lock up hoodlum coons. Roeland Street where jailbirds sing to the moon of sweethearts running around free: *My geliefde hang in die bos, my geliefde hang in die bos, my geliefde hang in die bitterbessiebos.*

Moses fishes in his deep pockets for the junkyard key.

Across the road Ou Piet Olifant stands on the veranda of the hotel, squinting his eyes at the Xhosa man and the white boy through the island of oleander and the mirage haze hanging over the tar. Empty tables are decked with plaid cloths and pink plastic flowers to lure travellers in.

Moses unlocks the padlock. The barbed gate swings and basking lizards scutter into the gaping eyeholes of broken headlamps. The junkyard is a graveyard of dented, gutted motorcars. A stray cat combs against my leg. I see the nodes of its arched backbone through its fur.

Moses points out an old, boxy Volvo. It is sky blue, but in patches it is the colour of the sea after an eclipse, churned rust red by the moon. The roof is caved in and the tyres flat, the rubber cracked dry under the sun. The Volvo stares at me, through one broken eye and one good eye, a sad old hobo of a motorcar begging to be painted, tuned and ridden.

Moses grins as he flicks a key to me. It catches the sun like a spinning coin. Out of instinct I want to call out: heads.

– The key was in the cubbyhole, Moses says.

I look at the husk of a motorcar and think she must feel lonely, stranded south in this desert place, so far from Sweden and her whizzing youth. I wonder if she came over the sea by ship and if she ever wove along the banks of a fjord, dodging moose or whatever kind of buck they have in Sweden. I realise I know nothing about Sweden, other than fjords and buck. And Björn Borg.

The seats, once the cherry red of the seams, are bleached pink. Wire springs snake out of the gashed back seat. I imagine she feels ashamed of her leaking guts and rusted husk.

I tap a tune on the dashboard. And Abba. I almost forgot Abba.

– So what do you say? smiles Moses.

– She'll do.

I can tell I have hurt his feelings.

– A coat of paint will perk her up, I add.

– Yes. And we can use the tyres from the jeep.

The jeep looks as if it was stamped to death by a rogue elephant avenging all the elephants who ended up as elephant-foot stools.

– I thought maybe we saw the roof off, Moses goes on. There has been no rain for two years. We just throw a canvas over at night.

I flinch. I am becoming like my mother, who could not bear to look when Byron, the gardenboy, hacked off branches from the coral tree when it reached too far over the lagoon road.

– So, you can see her on the road?

A hobo Volvo, jazzed up as a beach buggy on jeep wheels, bopping down Delarey with a black man and a white boy up front, and on the backseat a crazy bobtail dog biting at the wind.

– Ya. I can see her.

– Kulungile. I have only Sunday afternoons for working on the car. I need to sand it down and paint it and fix the engine. It growls but does not catch. And when you get your licence we drive down the N1 to Cape Town.

– But four years is forever.

– Forever for a boy, but years go by like river fish for an old man.

green apples

I drop from the window sill and hold my breath. Chaka does not stir. Just a cluck from the coop and the distant din of tin lids as the dustmen empty the bins on Delarey Straat. It is still dark, but there is a hint of mussel-shell pink and blue in the east. Fish-scale dew glints in the grass.

On the far side of town I hear the cargo train go *uloliwe ulo-liwe uloliwe*. This is the time Moses stirs to unlock the pumps. This is the time Marsden and I, rattled out of sleep by the milkman's clinking bottles, caught some waves before school.

Marika's backyard borders on the veld, miles and miles of bare veld. She climbs over the barbed wire, like a boy. Two horses graze the wet yellow grass. They lift their heads and stare at us, their jawbones shifting, as Marika walks up to them.

I hang back. Dirkie taught me to ride on the farm, but I am wary of horses: the way their nostrils flare and their muscles twitch randomly under a sleek hide, and the way they toss their heads to flick flies away from their wild black glassy eyes.

Marika whistles and the horses come to her. She combs her

fingers through the mane of the patchy horse and rubs the hard
bony ridge that runs down from his eyes to deep nostrils snorting
smokily in the cold air. Foam from yellow teeth comes off on the
white rugby jersey Marika has on. It has the number nine sewn on
the back. Some rugby boy must have given it to her. I am jealous. I
wonder if she kissed him.

– Climb on, she says.

At her words the front feet of the patchy horse do a skittery
dance. Marika whispers into his ear, a sound like the wind mur-
muring through bluegums.

– Are you sure he's tame?

– Come on. You're not scared, are you?

– It's just that I've never ridden bareback.

– As long as you're not scared. Horses smell fear, you know.

– I know.

I smile at Marika, and at the patchy horse, hoping she will not
see, and he will not smell, my fear.

– What's his name?

– Rogue, says Marika. Come on, before the sun comes up.

I hoist myself up on to Rogue's back and almost go over the
other side, but Marika catches my foot.

– Good. Just hold on.

The muddy horse has wandered away. She whistles for him.

– Hey, River, come boy, she says.

He comes to Marika. She reaches for his mane and swings
herself fluidly onto his back.

I focus on sending happy signals to Rogue, so he does not
throw me.

– You don't need to steer. Rogue will come after River.

She clicks her tongue a few times, as if rattling off a string
of Xhosa words, and her horse begins to run. Then Rogue, with

much sneezing and farting, jerks into a run. I cling to his mane and dig my heels in. I am joggled to and fro on his back, my ass coming down hard on his backbone. This has none of the poetry of the cowboy films. I would be glad to trade for a longboard, or a bicycle. Marika heads for an anthill and hurdles it. I brace myself for the jump, but at the last moment Rogue sidesteps and I am flung forward. I loop my arms around his neck.

– Whoooa whoooa, I call to him.

I am as scared as the time I braved the baboons for the Kodak film. I feel Rogue's shoulderblades under my hips and I sense how vulnerable I am compared to this animal rippling under me. I feel my hold slip. I know I am going to hit the earth hard. Rogue tosses his head to shake me off and I fall in a blur of tinted sky and pounding hooves and smell of horse. A hard thud and the world cartwheels and all I think is: the hooves, please God not the hooves against my head.

Then the sky is still and I feel nothing.

I hear Marika calling out:

– Douglas Douglas

Her head is upside down in the space of sky above me. The sun paints her skin orange. There is fear in her eyes.

– Douglas. You alright?

She scoops up my head into her lap. My shoulder begins to hurt.

– I'm fine.

– Jesus. I thought you said you could ride.

She kisses my eyebrow and picks grass out of my hair, like a mother monkey searching for ticks on her baby. I realise I do not know the word for a baby monkey. Monkey cub? Monkey kid? Monkey pup? I hear bubbles making a warbling music in Marika's stomach.

On the kerb, by our gate, Marika stares scared eyes at me as if my eyes might roll up white inside my skull as a doll's do when you tip it back.

– You sure you alright?

– Ya, I'm sure.

What I am not sure of is whether to kiss her or hug her. After lying with my head on her lap, it is now too casual just to say: so long.

– You should hug me, says Marika.

I hold my arms loosely around her. My face is in her hair and her hair smells of green apples. Thoughts of Marsden and my father begin to filter through strands of apple hair and I bury my head in deeper in the hollow of her neck and squinch my eyes to keep tears from coming.

I see Marsden on the beach, surfboard under his arm, turn to me and his skin is orange in the sun coming up over Hangklip and his teeth white as a cuttlefish or a seagull's breast. Then my father walks out of the sea mist. He puts his arm around Marsden's shoulders and says: the thing with you, Douglas, is your mind wanders. How will you ever play cricket for the province, if your mind wanders?

– Hey, I hear Marika's voice through layers of hair and memory.

I let go, feeling foolish and ashamed, and wish her goodbye.

– Totsiens, says Marika. She kisses me on the eyebrow again.

Halfway across the road she does a hopscotch hop, skip and jump. Then she turns to see if I am smiling.

And I am.

white girls

Marika and I walk down Delarey Straat to the Shell garage. Marika is in shorts and dirty white Dunlop tackies she has drawn blue daisies on with a pen. Butterflies dance in me as I wonder how Moses and Marika will get on, and what she will think of our rusty old junkyard Volvo.

When Moses catches sight of us, he stands up from his Black Label beer crate and pockets his yellow handkerchief.

– Ah, kunjani, Douglas. I see you have a friend. Kunjani, miss.

He bows and Marika twiddles the hem of her shorts. It is the first time I have seen her unsure.

– My pa does not want me to talk to blacks. He says blacks smell, and they rape white girls if they catch them in the veld. That's why he does not want me out by the reservoir.

Moses bows his head. I feel like burrowing under the earth.

– But I'm not scared, says Marika.

Moses tilts his old, scrubby head and looks deep into her eyes. I look up and down the road, hoping a motorcar will turn in for petrol, but nothing happens. Across the way, Ou Piet Olifant sits on the steps of the Rhodes Hotel, his head under a newspaper.

– Well, that is a something, Moses nods.

I sigh with relief.

– You okay? Marika asks me.

– It's just the sun. I need a drink. Do you want a cooldrink? A Coca-Cola, or something?

– A Fanta.

I fiddle in my pocket and find a coin among the coral seeds. One rand. As I go over to the icebox, I hear Marika say to Moses:

– You do not smell bad. Only of tobacco.

Moses finds this funny and laughs as he tips up a box for her to sit on.

– You know, my father does not let me drink fizzy drinks 'cause he thinks it is rude for a girl to burp.

I hear Moses laugh again.

I come back, ice-cold Coca-Cola and Fanta in hand, to find Marika sitting on the Black Label beer crate, sunning her bare legs. I remember Bessie Malan ranting: It is a crying shame the way the government lets blacks look over the railing at the white girls in the Muizenberg pool. No wonder they run around raping them. I wonder if Bessie changed her tune after the vagabond jumped the railing of the footbridge to save her. And I wonder how Marika can go on about blacks raping one moment and then kick off her Dunlops in front of Moses the next.

They laugh. I wish I had kept Moses to myself. I tap my Coca-Cola three times before tugging at the ring pull. Moses winks at me as I mimic his trick. Marika glugs down the Fanta in one long gurgling, gulping go. She burps, then flamingoes on the can with one foot. She taps the sides of the can with her fingers and the can concertinas flat. She picks it up and frisbees it over the jagged sharkteeth glass of the junkyard wall.

– Cool, hey?

– Cool, I say.

Though Oom Jan can crush a Coca-Cola can in his fist, I have never seen this trick before.

– Where do you come from? Marika asks Moses out of the blue.

– I come from the Transkei, Mandela's land.

– Did you ever assegai a man?

– Zulus stab with an assegai. Xhosas throw a spear. But I never killed a man.

– Pity, says Marika. I want to know how it feels.

– Who would you want to kill?

– Meneer de Beer, the teacher who makes us cut up lizards and other animals. Maybe Douglas told you about him?

– No.

Marika glances at me accusingly.

I shrug.

– I would love to assegai De Beer. And there is another man I would like to kill.

I stare at my sandals.

– I have seen men die, says Moses.

Marika is transfixed.

– It was on the mines. We heard the cries of the Zulu young men coming to make war. The young Xhosas went for their sticks from under the roof. We old men did not stop them, for their blood was on fire. They ran up to the wire. Some of the young men had guns. The police did not come until they lay in blood, Xhosa on this side and Zulu on the other. It is not something for a young girl to see.

Across the road, a rickety old Land Rover parks outside the hotel. Ou Piet Olifant comes out from under his newspaper. A man with a white goatee, khaki topi and khaki bermudas climbs out, as if climbing out of a Tintin comic. Ou Piet Olifant, all teeth, pulls out a chair for him. The goatee reminds me of the Kentucky man. I wonder if Kentucky will come to Klipdorp. Just a whiff of Kentucky would whisk my father back from the far shores of Malindi, and we would be a family again, squabbling over drumsticks and wings.

Thoughts of Kentucky go west as Joost cycles by. A pigeon flies after him. I laugh at the frantic flapping of the bird. Then I see the fishing gut glint in the sun. He has strung the bird to his saddle. Sometimes it flaps above his head, then it falls and the tar plucks a tail feather.

Marika jumps up and runs after him, yelling:

– Let the bird go, you bastard.

He pedals faster, the pigeon bobbing in his wake. Marika flags, then kneels in the street.

I run up to her. A feather flowers from her fingers. Her tears dot the tar.

A white, tail-finned Studebaker runs up onto the kerb and the door swings open. Marika's father jumps out, his brylcreemed hair slicked into grooves, his foot tapping.

– Wat maak jy in die straat? Waar is jou skoene? he barks at Marika.

Marika points at the garage, where her Dunlop tackies lie beside Moses' Black Label crate. Under the cobra gaze of Marika's father, Moses stands up.

Marika's father snatches Marika's arm and he rattles her as if he wants to free a fishbone caught in her gullet.

– I told you I don't want you hanging around kaffirs, or Cape Town kaffirboeties. Hoor jy my?

– One day I will go to the black township, Marika shouts at him. You can't stop me.

Marika's father backhands across the cheek. Her head flicks to the side. She faces him again, eyes defiant.

– I want to see.

Marika flinches as he lifts his hand again. He changes his mind.

– If you ever go to that damned Salem, that black hell, I'll beat you till you beg for mercy.

He says it slow, and in English. He wants Moses and me to catch each word. Then, as an afterthought, he mumbles:

– Haal jou skoene.

Marika goes to fetch her tackies. Moses picks them up and hands them to her. Then she comes back. She wipes her eyes with the back of her hand. She wants to say something to me but her father is revving the motor of the red-eyed Studebaker as if he is at Kyalami, waiting for the flag to drop. I stand there as the motor-car roars away. I feel sad that Marika did not see the Volvo, for though she still looks boxy and rusty, she is to carry Moses and me to the sea.

Moses and I go to the junkyard. I begin to sand the boot, while Moses jacks up the jeep to skive the deep-grooved wheels.

platanna zone

A Sunday afternoon in the backyard. The pepper tree props up a lazy sky. The neighbouring field is empty of rugby boys. Hope is kipping in the dark of her khaya. In the Karoo there is no water to spare for cooling the roof, so she has covered it with fanned palm leaves, held down by stones. The sun has sapped the leaves dry. I can just hear her ragged snores escaping the khaya dark, mingling with the clucking of cooped chickens. Chaka has burrowed into the cool sand under the pepper tree. My mother is painting.

I slide a brick under my longboard under the pepper tree. I stand on it and seesaw until I find my feet. I close my eyes.

I am riding a wave at Llandudno. I see shark-shadow kelp and rocks like dead seals under me. It is a good steady break and I bob and dip to pick up pace and stay with it. The Atlantic shouts in my ears and salt stings my eyes, but my mind is clear, as if a gust of wind blows through my head. It is a kif, tuned feeling and I want the wave to curve forever, before it barrels.

A volley of barks shoots me out of the sea and leaves me stranded in the Karoo, surfing the dry buffalo grass. Chaka clangs his claws against the fence. And beyond him, reaching her hand through the wire, is Marika. Chaka's bark catches in his throat as he smells her hand. His stub of a tail twitches and then his ass begins to swing. So much for my ferocious hunter dog.

She stands there barefoot, in a flowery cotton dress. She saw my jiggling songololo as I hopped across the rugby field. She saw me tumble from a horse. Now she sees me surfing a brick. I want to say something, but the words to justify all my jackassing do not come.

– You want to surf all afternoon, or do you want to come cycle out to the reservoir with me?

I hop down from the longboard.

– I thought your father didn't want you going out there.

– My father is out of town.

– I said I'd give Moses a hand with the car.

– Why do you always hang around him? Do you like him more than me?

I teeter on the brink of truth, then mouth a lie.

– No.

It does not convince her.

– Anyway, I'm going, she pouts, and spins on her heels.

– Wait, I'm coming. I jus' want to tell my mother.

I skip inside.

– Mom, I am going cycling with Marika.

– That's nice, Dee. Don't be late for tea, says my mother, dabbing oil at the canvas.

My heart is a flurry of birdwings beating against my ribcage. Surely she senses my high, but she goes on dabbing, eyes fixed to the canvas. Maybe she will glance up when the brush runs dry. But no, her eyes do not stray from the canvas, while the brush forays to the palette, twirls, muddying sunflower yellow with red, then flits back.

Dab dab dab. Flit. Twirl. Flit. Dab. The endless ritual of a mother bird spitting juiced goggas into yellow-rimmed, gaping pink beaks.

Outside again, I squint into the sunflared glare to make sure Marika is still there.

Along Mimosa Road Marika curves from one kerb to the other. I laugh at her, but I am too shy to mimic her. Besides, after falling from the ladder and from a horse, even something as instinctive as riding a bicycle seems charged with unforeseen risks. I keep an eye out for waylaying stones and potholes.

We turn off Mimosa into Reservoir Road. We cross two roads and then the tar gives out, and we are beyond kikuyu yards and yapping dogs and maids skindering over fences as they peel potatoes or unpeg clothes from the wire.

Down the dirt road, through jackalwire Karoo, I follow Marika, a weaving mirage. I am shadowed by a twang of guilt for jilting old Moses, perched alone on his Black Label beer crate under the mossie wire and the yellow fan of the Shell sign.

Stones, ploughed aside long ago, lie along the fence. Occasionally there is a Coca-Cola can among the stones, or a scrap of plastic snared on the wire, like some lonely flower. A hawk in a mimosa swivels its head as we go by and then turns its gaze to look for a flicker of life among the dead stones.

Dust filters up from the road and I taste it in my mouth.

Marika brakes to watch a leopard tortoise wade across the road.

Marsden and I get my father to stop Indlovu to pick up a dune tortoise on the Strandfontein road. We call him Tennessee, as he has a yawing, lopsided way of walking, as if he has sipped my father's Jack Daniel's Tennessee whiskey. One day Tennessee is gone. Marsden and I reckon my mother freed him. But my mother says no,

and Chaka has long ago given up hoping to lick him out of his shell.
Turns out Hope turned Tennessee into soup for a visit from some
long-lost Xhosa brother from the Ciskei. We dig Tennessee out of the
bin. Hope stands there, head bent in the shame of being caught out.
Marsden and I spin for him. I call heads, but Van Riebeeck does not
land face-up.

Marika sits on her heels like a peeing girl and folds her hands
on her lap. She shifts her heels to crab along after the tortoise.

– You know I meant it when I said I would assegai De Beer for
killing animals in his class.

Though I have given little thought to the cruelty of it, I
mouth:

– Ya, it's so inhuman.

I had thought Tennessee's death sad because I knew him, but
I never had qualms about shooting guineafowl on Oom Jan's farm
with Dirkie.

Chaka runs to the fallen bird and bites the head. He flicks the
screeching bird until it hangs limp from his grinning gob. Dirkie
runs up, tugs the bird away, and lops off its pink and light-blue head
with a bowie knife. He drops the head as a tip for Chaka. Chaka
trots after us with the lurid head cigarring from his lips.

I choose not to tell Marika. Instead, I swear:

– I will never dissect an animal in his class.

She looks up at me and squints her eyes, as if to say:

– We'll see.

I think of Meneer de Beer's long cane and wonder if lizards
count as animals. What about moles and rats? Surely Marika does
not think it cruel to kill rats? Maybe I can offer to dissect a rat
instead of a rabbit if Meneer de Beer calls me forward to bend.

We cycle on again, the zing of cicadas stinging my eardrum. Potholes carved out by long-ago rains. Not far along the

road Marika drops her bicycle in the dust. The front wheel spins the sound of a fishing reel. She goes up to the fence to study the skeleton of a lizard hanging on the wire.

– A jacky hangman, she says.

A jacky hangman butcher bird barbed it to dry out in the sun and never came back for it. Maybe a farmboy potted the bird off a telegraph wire. Surely spiking a lizard on barbed wire is just as cruel as stabbing a lizard with a compass? But Marika says:

– Isn't it beautiful?

I nod, though I'm not so sure.

Marika lifts her dress to take a screwed-up tissue out of her white panties. She unfolds the tissue and then gingerly unhooks the skeleton. She wraps it in the tissue and lays it in the flat-kit pouch that swings under her bicycle seat.

I wonder if she just wears white panties on weekends, or if she sometimes secretly wears white underneath at school.

– I once found a snakeskin in the veld, she says. You can come and see it sometime.

– Thanks.

I have never cared much for dead animals. The elephant-foot stool always gave me the creeps. But my eyes begin to scour the veld beyond the fence for snakeskins and skeletons in the hope of finding something for her. I remember how I used to search the rocks for periwinkle for my mother. Guilt flinks like a fish through a deep, murky pool in my mind.

My father's voice echoes in my head: First one to spot a lion gets ten cents.

Perhaps I will find Tennessee if I dig in the Indian teaboxes railed up from Muizenberg.

We go on, a dead lizard in her pouch. We cycle around Jakkalsdraai Koppie and there is the reservoir. Not a bluewater palm oasis, just a round, brick dam of tea-coloured water, five foot deep. The reservoir reminds me of an unthatched Xhosa rondavel. A spidery shadow is cast across it by the still blades of a steel windmill.

Marika rests her bicycle against the drinkwater sloot. She dips her head under water, then flings her wet hair up. Strands of her hair curl like octopus tendrils. I laugh and she squirts a jet of water at my face. I laugh again, but I am not sure I should do the same to her. While I waver, Marika scoops up water in her hands and pours it onto the clay sand beside the sloot. The thirsty earth drinks it in fast.

– For the frogs, she says.

I laugh again, thinking she is kidding me.

– They suck up water out of the sand through their skin. It's called osmosis.

I remember my father telling me that there are fish that survive years under the dry cracked floor of dams and rivers. My father called them phoenix fish, as they wriggle out of the sand when the rain falls, the way the phoenix, after flaming to ashes, feathers to life again. The thought of fish and frogs and other throbbing things I have not dreamed of under my feet spooks me. I hope Marsden, who hides in reflections and shadows, does not skulk down below: a cold-skinned, blind throbbing.

Then she lies down flat, her ear against the clay sand, as if she can hear the frogs osmosing down under.

I peer over the brim of the reservoir and touch the water. It is cold after the water of the sloot.

Then she is on her feet again. There is sand on her dress.

– Turn around, she says.

So I turn to gaze at the Karoo veld: just a few dips and koppies, like the moon.

I spin around when I hear a splash. There lies her dress on the sand.

She surfaces and says:

– It's so lekker. Come in.

Standing close to the wall so Marika does not see me, I peel off my shorts and underpants together.

I toe up the wall and teeter bare-assed on the brim. I am not sure whether to flip in backwards, like a diver from the rim of a Zodiac, or to twist to drop in head first. Either way Marika is going to see my songololo, close up.

– Come on, there are no crocs, teases Marika.

I can tell she is enjoying my awkwardness. I go for the Zodiac flip and sink down into the cool water tapped from a deep under-world river. The sun spears through the dusky water and I can see her stomach and legs, the colour of the underbelly of a frog. I see a smudge of black down by her hips, like a Chinese brushflick on canvas. I surface into the blue sky and the laughter spilling from Marika's teeth.

– Lekker, hey? she says, spitting water at me.

This time I dare to spit back at her. She yelps and lunges away, floating her budding, nubby breasts.

– It's my favourite place in the world. I hate going to the public pool.

– Me too.

Until I saw Marta in her bikini with the watermelon motif, I never went to the public pool in Muizenberg, so bound by railings and rules. The sea was free. The reservoir is hardly a sea but still I get the feeling of floating, severed from the world. In the sea it is a feeling mingled with the fear of sharks and razor rocks. In the reservoir the feeling is mixed with a fear that Marika will laugh at my songololo, shrunk to a stub in the cold water. It just pulls back like a touched sea anemone.

Marika dives under and her feet periscope out of the water. She handwalks along the floor of the reservoir, and her feet follow.

I dive down and my feet go up. They drift apart like twins out of synch. Each foot wants to go finning away alone. I stay down, fighting to pull them together. I surface, spluttering.

– How do you stay up on your surfboard with such awful balance? laughs Marika.

– I surf on my feet, I say.

Not revealing that a longboard is a barge of a surfboard and that balancing on it is hardly a circus act. You can beach a longboard like a canoe, because it does not sink as you slow down.

– So, seaboy, how long can you stay under water?

– I'm not sure. Maybe two minutes.

– Go under and I'll count one kangaroo, two kangaroo. Okay?

– Okay.

I dive under. For a while I enjoy the cool and her white skin, ghostly under the water like a photographic negative. I wonder how many kangaroos I have been down for. I shut my eyes to focus on taming my heartbeat and slowly uncorking bubbles. I drift in a black platanna zone.

Two minutes maybe.

My empty lungs burn and I see red behind my eyelids. Psychedelic sea anemones reel in a red sea. I kick out my feet and skin my toes.

I suck in deep draughts of sky and hang on to the brim while my heart beats a runaway tomtom beat.

Marika is out of the pool with her dress on over wet skin. Again she laughs at me, gasping platanna. I see the shadow of nipples under cloth. Marika swings her head to dry her tassled hair, the way a dog coming out of the sea shakes sea water and wetdog smell in your face.

Behind her I see her white panties caught on the spiderweb
spokes of her bicycle wheel. A breeze catches the cloth and the
wheel turns a quarter turn.

The blood on my toes begins to crust.
    – How long have you been in the Karoo? I ask Marika.
    – Forever, says Marika. I was born in Klipdorp.
    – Have you ever been away?
    – Just to Durban, for a holiday. Pa is always travelling, but he
never takes me or Ma. Sometimes he gets drunk on his quarts of
Hansa beer and hits Ma. In the morning, all babbalaas, he goes
down on his knees and begs her to forgive him. Vergewe my,
vergewe my, he sobs. And she says if Jesus forgives her, how can
she not forgive him. But why would Jesus need to forgive her? All
she does all day is read the *Huisgenoot,* keeping one eye on the
maid to see she mops and does not burn the pots.
    Marika picks up a stone and chucks it at the windmill. It
clangs against the steel.
    – I sometimes think of running away but there is nowhere
in this desert to run to. And if you hitch, you end up raped or
stabbed, or kidnapped by the Arabs.
    Marika, eyes veiled by the kind of beaded cloth you cover a
jug with to keep the flies out the milk, jikas her hips in my head.
    – I once cycled out here, to the reservoir, with a blanket and
a tin of Ouma rusks to camp out. I dipped the rusks in the coffee I cooked on the fire. Then I lay down, under the stars, and
thought, this is the life: just me and the stars and fire and no sulk-
ing mother or sourpuss teachers.
    Another stone zings off a windmill blade.

– I lay there until I heard a sound in the dark, just outside the firelight. It was the sound of teeth cracking bone and I was scared. Then I saw his eyes shine in the firelight and I thought: I am dead. It's a leopard. Please God, make the leopard go away, I begged. But eyes stared fire at me. I jumped on my bike and pedalled like crazy. After a while I turned around and saw it was not a leopard after me, but a lynx. I dropped my bike to pick up stones to chuck at him. He dodged the stones. When I got on my bike again, he followed me.

The lynx lopes after Marika, across the horizon of my imagination. She drops her panties in the sand, and he stoops to sniff at them.

– Only when I rode under the orange lamps of Reservoir Road, did the lynx spin around and go back into the dark.

He slinks back to the dying coals to pick up the abandoned bones that have to do instead.

– When I got home Ma cried and Pa beat me with his belt until I bled. Then he begged me to forgive him. I spat at him and ran to my room. I smeared the blood on the sheet so my mother would see. Afterwards, as I lay on the bloodied sheet, I wondered if the lynx would have eaten me, or lain down by me under the mimosa. I wished I had chanced it with the lynx rather than running home to my doos of a Pa.

My hand stings. I uncurl my fist to find I have cut my palm with the blade of my father's Swiss Army pocket knife. Marika is so deep in her thoughts, she does not see. I lick the blood.

– He's still your father, I tell her.

– You know, he makes me sick. One time I heard a sound like a cat lapping milk and peeped through the toilet keyhole to see Pa wanking over the *Scope* magazine. I wish he was dead, or sailed away like your pa.

Marika's disgust at her father's lust makes me feel uneasy. I recall how my father told Marsden and me he had seen a snake in Bangkok slither inside a woman's sex, how it somehow found its way out again, head first. I wonder if he saw other things he never dared tell his boys.

– I want to travel the world when I get out of school, says Marika. I want to backpack through Europe, but Pa says it is the backpack girls who end up smoking dagga in Amsterdam and not shaving their armpits and whoring around.

– I love my father, I tell her.

– Hey, I'm sorry. But maybe your pa did not hit you, hey?

– Sometimes he did. I remember one afternoon, in Muizenberg, my brother and I were in the mood for monkeying around, so we teased Byron, the gardenboy, hoping he would drop his hoe and chase us. He was hoeing up the dried-out pumpkin vines. If he dug deeper he would unearth the skeletons of all the dogs my father buried over the years. Inye, zimbini, zintathu, we chanted to the tune of *eeny meeny miny mo*. Inye, zimbini, zintathu, catch a nigger by his toe, if he hollers let him go, inye, zimbini, zintathu. My father came out of his outhouse study with a tennis shoe in his hand. We bolted for the house. My father caught Marsden on the backdoor steps. I heard the thwacking of the tennis shoe on Marsden's ass as I skidded into the kitchen. Hope was clattering away at the sink, the Sunlight foam flying. My mother was always telling her to go easy on the Sunlight. I dived for the curtained cupboard under the sink and skimmed along the waxed boards under Hope's skirt. I had my knees under my chin. Fish heads eyed me from the dustbin. I heard the clatter and clank of china on the draining-board and felt the U-bend pipe dig into my ribs. I heard my father's feet creak the boards. Have you seen Douglas? my father demanded of Hope. My stomach churned with fish stink and fear. No, Master, Hope said.

– The same maid you have now? Marika wants to know.

– The same Hope. She breastfed Marsden and me because my mother's milk ran dry before we had drunk our fill. Her boy September was born six months before, so she still had milk. Anyway, she said: No, master. Then I heard my father's footsteps fade. From somewhere deep in the house I heard my father calling me. I darted out from under the sink and headed for the door. Out in the yard, Marsden yelled: Run, Doug, run. And I ran, Chaka snapping at my flying heels. The front gate was just up ahead when my ribs thudded against the grass. My father was on top of me. The rubber sole of the Dunlop tackie stung like blazes.

Marika twirls some strands of her hair into a string and chews on it.

I throw a stone at the windmill. It flies soundlessly into the setting sun.

– Afterwards, my father told us he never wanted to hear us call a black man *nigger* again because it was as rude as *kaffir*. Casting my eyes down in shame I saw Dunlop tattooed on my skin where my father missed my ass. He said we had to say sorry to Byron. Byron said: Kulungile, boys. I know you good boys.

Marika kisses me on the cheek. My heart flies a boomerang loop around the windmill.

– Come, she says. We better go home.

She picks her panties off the spokes and pulls them on under her dress.

⌒

I drop my bicycle in the grass amid a concert of crickets and a yammer of distant dogs under the Southern Cross, the foot slanting south to where the Atlantic and Indian run together.

Under the stars in Malindi: ice clinks in the whiskey in my

father's hand on a stoep on the edge of the sea, and in his head whirl memories of me.

Through the kitchen window I see my mother alone at the table. She has peeled the red hog's head off a bottle of Gordon's London Dry Gin. *Doctor Zhivago* lies face down. When she sees me in the open doorway, she hurls a tea caddy at me. It jangs off the door jamb and scatters tea over the chessboard lino.

Chaka barks and skids across the floor in that foggy, foreign moment before he knows it is me.

– Where on earth have you been? my mother yells.

Chaka, cowed, ducks under the table.

– I was out cycling with Marika, I stammer at the violence of her voice.

– I've been worried sick.

– I'm sorry, I mumble, on the verge of tears.

Her voice mellows:

– Dee, it would kill me if something happened to you. You must promise me always to come home for tea.

Since we lived in Camden my mother calls supper tea, even if there is no tea to drink. I sulk and stare down at my sandals, islands in a sea of tea leaves. I wonder if you can smoke tea.

Marsden and I overhear a UCT student on the train tell another that smoking the strings from under banana skins gives you a high, so we dry banana skins on the roof. Behind the cabins on the beach, we slit one of my Dad's cigarettes and spill the tobacco onto a square of Cape Times *and mix in strands of dry banana. We forget to roll in a filter and end up spluttering and spitting out tobacco on the sand.*

– I promise to be home for tea.

Chaka, sensing the coast is clear, surfaces again, wagging his stub. It was a joke, right? I knew it was a joke, he grins.

– I'm sorry I flew off the handle, Dee.

She gets up and comes to me. I think she is going to hold me and I want her to, but she just gives me a butterfly kiss on the forehead and floats past me into her studio.

– Dee, I need you to be good to me, you understand?

I nod.

– Be a dear and make your mother a g&t.

I go into the kitchen and pour gin from the naked bottle. The Indian tonic is lukewarm, so she will want it on the rocks. My fingers stick to the tin of the ice tray and I have to hold the tray under cold water to free them again. My hand stings under the flow.

I go back into the studio with the ice going *clink clink* in the glass, and a cube in my mouth. My mother has her head in her hands and I think she is crying but she tilts her head up and whisks hair out of her eyes.

– Dee, come sit beside me.

I join her on the old riempie bench she has in the studio.

– I remember so vividly when you were born. You and Marsden lay crying on my stomach, covered in blood. I sang *Blowin' in the Wind* to you. I had sung it you while you were still in my womb, and you both hushed as if you remembered the song. The first few days I couldn't tell you apart, but you were Douglas and Marsden by the time we went home to the flat in Sea Point. Marsden, always sweet, would doze when he'd drunk his fill, but you were moody and needed rocking and singing. You would only fall asleep with your head nooked between my breasts.

Rather than look into my mother's eyes, I stare at the stinging slit in my palm. A toothless red zip.

– You and Marsden were the fruit of my love, and though I sometimes yearned for lost freedom, I loved you with all my soul. Dee, you have to take care. If I lost you, I'd have no reason to go on.

It seems unfair, in a world of hard balls and sharks and lynxes,

to expect me to outfoot all the dangers fate throws my way. The
weight of having to survive for my mother bears down on me. I
wish my father would come and put up his feet and read the *Cape
Times*. I would know then, as the ice clinked in his Jack Daniel's,
that I was free to run out into the dark to play fearlessly, just as I
had swum freely in a sea of dancing kelp shadows when he was
just a stone's throw away.

nagapie eyes

I carry the image of Marika through the jostle and jangle of school. In my mind I see beads of amber water on her skin. In a hazy dwaal, I snag my shoulder bone against the bones of others. Smudged sounds filter through a film of sweet illusion.

My desk in Meneer de Beer's class is scarred by graffiti, furrowed by nibs and pocket knives. Indian blue ink has seeped into the wood. There is a hole from the days of inkwells and a groove to keep HB pencils from rolling down the slant of the desk. Under the flip-up lid: hard, dry tits of gum. Some boy has gouged out the word *fuck*. In my mind fucking is an impaling, a spearing. My love for Marika is too pure to want to fuck her. I want to dream her, colour her in.

Meneer de Beer's voice, on the sexuality of the avocado, rambles on. I gaze nagapie eyes at Marika. Though I yearn for her to glance at me, to signal to me that the reservoir was a beautiful thing, she stares ahead, chews a stubby pencil.

In my mind she drifts alone across a desert of shifting dunes. Her footmarks flower in the sand. A mangy lynx lopes after her. It wants the water on her skin.

Marika sucks in her lips and then blows them out at me with a pop sound and a widening of her eyes. The pop of her lips is the pop of a bluebottle on the beach when you jab it with a mussel shell. My heart tumbleturns. She loves me.

Meneer de Beer drops his chalk. He bends for it and his tortoise-shell glasses slip from his bent-down head. He crushes the chalk underfoot as he fumbles with blind fingers through a fog of laughter.

An image surfaces out of the developing paper of my mind: Moses' hands flapping in the dust, a hopeless reaching for his stolen pass.

Meneer de Beer's glasses lie at my feet and I instinctively pick them up to hand to him.

I glance at Marika. She tongues the tip of her nose. She loves me not.

Then the glasses are in Meneer de Beer's palm. In that instant before hanging them on the bridge of his nose, he squinches his eyes at us like a dazed mole unearthed by a dog. Then his eyeballs focus through the lenses and the class falls silent. He is the teacher again.

A crow pecks at its reflection in the windowpane, a waxy oilslick glint in its feathers.

– Thank you, boy, says Meneer de Beer.

Someone from the rows of desks behind me makes the sound of a plughole spinning water down, but quits when Meneer de Beer glares at the class. Joost sniggers and he is called to the front. Joost bends over the desk, his grey shorts spanning taut. Meneer de Beer chalks his cane. It is a custom of his, to prove his skill.

Each cut is a crack in my ears, the sound of Hope beating the dust out of carpets hung over the fence, the sound of distant shots.

A man falls in the dust of running feet. Before my father can blinker my eyes with his hands, I see red squirt from the man's head.

A shudder runs down Joost's spine as he stands and I know he is biting down the pain. Sure enough the cane leaves four equally spaced lines on Joost's grey shorts. As he walks back to his desk he glares at me, as if I am to blame.

The bell goes for lunch and I gather my books and run out, confused. Hope has made a sandwich for me but I cycle home anyway, to escape Joost's revenge and Marika's teasing.

⤚

Hope is pegging out the washing, singing a song she used to sing when she tutuzela'd me on her back as a baby. I stand there under the pepper tree and cry with longing for something lost, while her song ripples through me. I feel sure I remember the cocooned feeling of being tutuzela'd. I wish I could crawl back into a fuzzy pouch and not have to decipher all the signals in the world around me.

Chaka stirs from his guineafowl dreams and bounds up to me, dock wagging and drool dangling. As we run up the steps, I hear Hope call after me.

– Master Douglas, don't go inside.

I just laugh, thinking she does not want Chaka dirtying her waxed floors.

In the kitchen, beheaded fish swim in the sink. Their heads lie in a bucket. Marsden and I used to finger the fish eyes, but now I feel faint. I tug Chaka's head out of the bucket. No doubt Hope will want to brew a soup with the heads.

Chaka growls as we go into the front room and I clutch at

his collar. A black woman, naked below an orange turban, stands beyond my mother's easel. Before my eyes adjust to the shade, the woman reaches for a cloth. Chaka barks and the hair along his spine porcupines. My mother lays her brush down in the groove of the easel. Chaka licks her hand and wags his stub. She gives me a kiss on the forehead. I feel conscious of the eyes under the orange turban.

– Dee, honey. Is something wrong at school?

– No. I just forgot a book.

As I go, dragging Chaka after me, I glance back to see the cloth fall. I glimpse a messy mossie nest of black hair down by her hips.

Outside again, Hope smiles:

– Ulungile?

– Ndilungile, I say. Sure I'm fine.

I am not in the mood for Hope's Black Cat peanut-butter sandwich, so I cycle to the Sonskyn Kafee to buy a packet of Fritos chips. On the paving outside the café sits a club-footed man, begging. I fish out Hope's peanut-butter sandwich. He reaches out his hands and says:

– Dankie, my baas.

As I go through the curtain of fly beads, I glance back to see the beggarman pulling the two thick slices of bread apart to study the inside.

In the café dark, as things slowly come into focus, I see the café tannie, her elbows on the counter. She licks her fingers to flick through the pages of a magazine. From behind her an old man stares out of the shadows, his skin as grooved as elephant skin. A fly drinks the liquid in the corner of his eye, but he ignores it. As I go out, Fritos in hand, his eyes follow me, though his head stays stock-still.

Outside again, the beggarman holds out the bread to me.

– Peanut butter is not for me, he says.

I have no choice but to take the sandwich back.

I look around to see if anyone has seen me take bread from a beggar. Further along, two coloured girls swing a rope, while a third skips. I hear them chanting: beechie, chappie, bubblegum, lick my bum. Fortunately they are too caught up in the game to see me.

– But I laaik Fritos, says the beggarman.

So I part with my packet of tomato-flavour Fritos. I look at the dirt under his fingernails as he rips the Fritos open and know that there is no way I am going to eat the sandwich now, but my mother has taught me never to throw good food away. I get back on my bicycle, the sandwich in one hand, and cycle down the street towards school, eyes skinned for a dog that looks as if it might gulp peanut butter.

No dogs. Guiltily, I ditch it in a dustbin.

After school, I creep into my mother's studio to look at the painting. The wet oilpaint glistens. Her nipples are black peaks on coffee-coloured koppies. Her stomach blends into dry, cracked desert mud, as if she has come out of the earth. I am tempted to scrape the surface, to see if the mossie nest is there: a sketched impression, under the layered mud of oilpaint.

Moses is pumping diesel into a dented old Bedford with the licence plate wired on and the windscreen spiderwebbed from a kicked-up stone.

Though Moses sees me, his eyes stay on the pump. He stops at 60 rands and 2 cents. It is not his style to tap fuel beyond the round number, even by 2 cents. I can tell by the way he shakes the last drops out of the hose that he is cross with himself. Some of the drops run down the dusty flank of the Bedford.

It is only after the Bedford has backfired a cloud of grey smoke and lurched back out onto the road that Moses turns to me.

– I waited for you all afternoon, young baas.

He has not called me young baas for a long time.

– I'm sorry. I was going to come but Marika came by, and I went swimming with her.

Moses drops his head and wipes his hands with his yellow handkerchief. He rubs his hands hard, as if they are stained with paint or blood. It makes me want to cry.

– I'm sorry, Moses.

An Alfa 2000 swerves in. The bucket seats are so deep that the man inside is dwarfed. My father drove an Alfa 2000 until Marsden and I were born. My father used to say: I could pack everything I had in the world into my Alfa. My Dylan and Slowhand records, my cricket togs, my surfboard on the roof. But having twins ended the freewheeling, happy-go-lucky days.

– Fill her up, the Alfa driver snaps at Moses.

– Yes, baas, says Moses.

I pick up my bicycle. I would like to tell him that the Cape Town dream means as much to me, but I know if Marika calls for me again next Sunday I will go with her. Besides, it is a pipe dream. He has no pass, never mind a licence. And how am I going to learn to drive when Indlovu rusts away in the garage and my mother hardly ever drifts away from her easel?

I find my mother at the kitchen table with Hope. I avoid my mother's eyes out of guilt that I stole back to gawk at the painting.

But my mother does not pick it up. She is in a festive mood.

– Come, Dee, have some champagne. Lina wrote to say she sold one of my paintings for 400 pounds. Can you imagine it? Remember I sent a few rolled-up canvases to Lina? Well, she found a man on Portobello Road who wanted *Karoo Dusk*. Four hundred pounds he paid for it. And he wants to see more of my work.

She pours champagne into a glass and it fizzes over onto the tablecloth. Instead of reaching for a dishcloth, Hope just giggles. The champagne is from Oom Jan's farm. Every day for three years the bottles are given a twist by black hands.

I sip champagne and keep it in my mouth for the fizz on my tongue. I can hardly believe anyone would pay for a painting my mother has painted. She is just a teacher who has abandoned the blackboard. Besides, the sky in the painting is the fake pink-orange dusk of a cowboy film and the windmill looks like a big flower. Still, my mother is on cloud nine.

– Lina says the dealer loves the untamed, aboriginal feel to it.

Well, that proves this Portobello man is crazy. He thinks the Karoo is the Australian outback.

My mother's breasts dangle freely under her caftan. When she drinks I see tufts of black hair under her arm. It fazes me, as I have never seen her unshaven there, and I wonder if it means she does not care about being pretty anymore. I can't imagine Miss Forster would let herself go. In my daydreams of Amsterdam, the cafés are brimful and the coffee never runs dry. Through the haze of voices and smoke Miss Forster's mouth leaves red lipstick on the lip of a white espresso cup.

fluke

Chaka barks and barks. I yell at him out of my bedroom window, but he goes on barking. I jump out of the window, go around to the granadilla-entwined front gate. Chaka is barking at the dominee, the pastor from the Dutch Reformed church. I grab Chaka by the neck to still him.

– Good afternoon, dominee.

Behind me I hear my mother and Hope giggling over their champagne.

– Afternoon. I want a word with your mother, if I may.

As he mouths his words the tuft of a beard on his chin wags, as if he is a chewing goat. Chaka growls at the wagging beard, convinced it is some kind of ratty animal.

I go back to the kitchen, dragging Chaka behind me.

– The dominee is at the gate. He wants you.

My mother hiccups, goes to the tap, dips her face under the jet of water, and dries it with a tea towel.

– Keep Chaka inside. I shan't be long.

Hope, out of habit, runs water into the sink for the glasses. I go through the kitchen to my room, shut Chaka inside and jump out the window. I edge around the house until I hear the dominee:

– It is not that I beg you to come to worship, but that you have some understanding for the way the folk think.

In my mind I see his tufty, ratty beard wagging.

– You see, it is expected of a woman in mourning to be, let me say, retiring. How are folk to make sense of the naked paintings when I myself find it hard to understand?

– But no one needs to make sense of them, my mother laughs. I paint in my own house and, if they are ever exhibited, it'll be far away.

– But, lady, if you have to paint such, how may I phrase it?, such stirring pictures, can you not paint a white? Forgive me for being so frank, but you must know folk find it disturbing enough to picture naked skin under your brush, never mind bare black skin.

– Dominee, you send me a white girl from your flock and I'll paint her naked white skin for you.

My mother has a cross edge to her voice. I peer around the corner to catch the sorrowful look of the dominee.

– You know, Mrs Thomas, a woman with your tragic story ought to turn to God, wags his chin.

– Dominee, a woman with my story ought to mistrust God.

– You know not what you say, the dominee whispers.

My mother spins her head to frown at me for eavesdropping. I duck into shadow. Damn. I wonder how she sensed it.

Facing the dominee again, she says:

– Dominee, I know what I feel.

She turns away from him, and then changes her mind.

– Dominee, what are the chances of a boy being killed by a cricket ball? Have you ever heard of such a thing happening? A fluke, a freak accident, one may call it. But when the chances are so remote of the ball hitting just the spot, the Achilles' heel of the head, then you begin to wonder if it is not somehow miraculous.

The dominee winces.

– Madam, surely you do not accuse God of murder?

– Of which murder? The murder of his son? The murder of my son? The murder of the Jews? Of the children in Soweto?

– Well, I bid you good day then. No doubt you have suffered. I will pray for you, and for the boy. Perhaps for his sake you will not harden your heart forever against God.

– Good day, dominee.

– Good day, Mrs Thomas.

james dean

I find a postcard on my pillow. My mother used to leave gifts for Marsden and me on our pillows after shopping: sometimes a box of Smarties, sometimes an Archie comic, once a Toto record we had begged for. She has not done it for a long time and just the sight of something lying on my pillow squeezes tears from my eyes.

It is a black-and-white photograph of James Dean, his eyes just peeping out of his jersey. The photograph is marred because the post office carelessly franked it. My heart skips a beat as I flick it over. It is from Mister Skinner. Why would old Skin write to me?

Dear Douglas

You are often on my mind. I would love to know how you are, out there in the Karoo. I imagine it is another world. Having lived in the city for so long, I am unnerved by such vast space. I am an incurable townsman, but you are young and can adapt. I never imagined, when I took you to the Hard Rock, that fate had another cruel act in store for you.

My tears blur the writing and I have to stop reading. I sit down on the orange sofa and flick the postcard over again to stare at James Dean. I wonder if he had an inkling, when the photo was snapped, that Death was lurking just down the road, waiting to leap out at his Spyder like a shark-fanged baboon, like a fiery-eyed tokoloshe?

I read on.

I still have an essay on Gatsby *you handed in to me. It's rather good. Maybe you will go on to write, like your father. Perhaps, one day, I will open the* Cape Times *to find the byline, Douglas Thomas, your name.*

Yours
Philip Skinner

I fold the postcard and pocket it. I recall his feathery touch, and see now it was lust as much as pity. Lust snuffed out by the whistle of the Cape Town train. There is a tapping at the window. A pigeon pecks at his reflection.

malindi

I find a spare headlamp glass in the jungle gym of junkyard cars, and the Volvo has two good eyes again.

I sand down the rust husk of the roofless Volvo, so we can paint her. I want to paint her a buttercup yellow with pink and green flowers like the surfer van my father and mother had when they were young in Sea Point. The reedy voice of Joan Baez singing *Blowin' in the Wind* comes over the radio.

Under the Camps Bay palms of long ago, my father is the harmonica longing to touch her, my mother the guitar, skipping just out of reach.

Moses does not mind the colour, so long as she hums along the road. For him it is all tuning and timing. He is forever searching the bands for a radio signal on the car radio that he salvaged from the junkyard. He tilts the radio and fiddles with the aerial until the static fades out and music sings through sweetly. Sometimes it takes a good five minutes to find unmuddy music.

After sanding the afternoon away to the Soweto vibes from the car radio, I want to wash my hands. Moses goes with me around to the back of the garage, to use the sink and soap in his room.

The outside of Moses' room is festooned with relics salvaged from dead motorcars. Flotsam strung on fishing gut from the gutter, fetish dolls and bones and beads and feathers that hung from rearview mirrors. Strings of threaded shells chime in the breeze. A Barbie doll swings nakedly, short of a leg like Hans Christian Andersen's tin soldier. Pink geraniums overflow hanging beach-buckets. Saint Christopher wades through a river with Jesus clinging on like a monkey. Just so, Marsden and I were blanketed up and carried tutuzela-tutuzela on Hope's back.

In the shade of a beach umbrella, milk yellows in the lid of a Cobrawax tin. A zizzing fly drowns in the sour liquid.

– For the junkyard cats, says Moses. They come to my door for milk when the sun goes under. Six or seven at a time lap up the milk, jowl to jowl. It is a beautiful thing to see. At night, sometimes, they creep in through my window and lie on my bed. Sometimes they fight on the roof and I jump awake at the screaming. I am afraid the tokoloshe has come for me. But it is only the cats and I shoo them out. His laugh gurgles up from a deep well in his stomach.

I laugh too, at the thought of Moses jumping out of his skin when the banshee yowl of junkyard cats jerks him out of his dreams. Before the mist of sleep clears, the dwarfgoblin tokoloshe bays for blood.

A shaft of dusty sun falls on a dangly-eyed panda on a bed high on bricks to outwit the stubby tokoloshe. The panda watches skewly as I dip under the veil of flowers, into the cool dark of the room.

In a corner, on a Cadac gas stove, is a pot of caked putu.

Over the sink is a broken mirror, tinted green like a fish tank. I scrub my hands, then bend to drink water from the tap. Fish eyes blink at me from the plughole. I look up and Marsden stares back at me. His eyes are like pebbles in the liquid green. Water beads down his forehead into his eyes, so close in the mirror I want to lick it away.

My eyes flick across to the reflection of Moses in the doorway, and back to the mirror again, but Marsden is gone and all I see is me, lips chapped by the Karoo sun and the skin scratched raw in the dent of my chin.

A motorcar hoots.

– I must go, says Moses.

He goes out, leaving me alone. I am scared to look deep into the mirror again, in case Marsden's face swims up out of the green. I am not sure how to tell my brother I sometimes forget I am a twin.

At school in Cape Town teachers sometimes confused Marsden and me. I did not mind because for me where Marsden ended and I began was undefined. His mind and mine shuttlecocked back and forth. Sometimes I was Marsden: artist. I saw the magic of a seagull's feather through his eyes. And then I was me again: staring out the train window, dreaming of how Miss Forster's milk-white breasts billowed under her buttons. A knowing glance from Marsden would reveal my vision lay bare before his eyes and I would wish I had the freedom to dream untapped dreams.

Now, untwinned, untwined, I dream untapped dreams, of Marika, of Amsterdam, and of my father in Malindi.

I see my father on a beach. Smoke spirals up from a cigarette, dangling from the corner of his mouth. He sharpens a pencil with a pocket knife, and the shavings fall to the sand. A breeze picks up and whisks the shavings away. He sips coffee from a thermos flask, sunk in the sand. Then he begins to write along the edge of a newspaper. This is what it is like to write a book, cigarettes and pencil shavings, newspapers and coffee. He looks up and winks at

me. The words come hard, like reeling in a hooked fish on a handline, hand over hand.

    – Hey, dad. It was fate. It wasn't your fault.

    – My boy, I know. But a hard fate to ride, hey?

He laughs a bitter, lonely laugh.

albino monkey

Another typical Sunday afternoon in Klipdorp. Time drags. Moses sits on his Black Label beer crate, eating bread and chips. He washes the bread and chips down with Stoney ginger beer. I drown the mamba tube of my bicycle in a drum of water, looking for the telltale bubbles of a hole made by a devil thorn. My grandfather brought the bicycle over from England and some of the patches mark the days he cycled there, through seas of green. Other patches, orange-edged, are from the glass of dropped cooldrink bottles on the road from Muizenberg to Kalk Bay. Still others from fruitbin nails on Oom Jan's farm.

On the car radio, Miriam Makeba sings with the Skylarks. Her voice floats over the tin sound of the guitar and the tapping of the drums. And higher still than her voice, the pennywhistle glides like a swift dipping and looping in the sky.

– Miriam is in exile, but they still chance her songs on the radio, Moses tells me.

On Sundays in Muizenberg, Hope sat on the doorstep, clicking a long-toothed comb through her spongy hair while the radio played black jazz. On Sundays we went for long drives in Indlovu, east along the sea-road to Hermanus to screwdriver black mussels from the rocks, or inland to Oom Jan's farm for a braai and sweet potatoes and a swim in the dam. My father tuned in to Radio 5: Fleetwood Mac or the Eagles or Simon and Garfunkel. Good road music, my father called it. But you never heard black African jazz on Radio 5.

And when my father was in a good mood he would tell us stories as we went along:

There once was a slaveboy called Naartjie, because his face was as sweet as the juice of a naartjie. He was so beautiful that all the slavegirls of the Boland wanted him and would lift up their skirts to show him their legs, strong from tramping grapes barefoot, like the legs of hockey girls.

My father was always teasing my mother about her strong legs from all the years she played hockey. He told Marsden and me that he had to fork out a big lobola for his woman. James, please, my mother would beg. But my father would go on regardless.

But Naartjie, he didn't flutter an eyelid at their legs, so they lifted their skirts higher.

My father would slide my mother's skirt up her legs and she would smack his hand away and Marsden and I would giggle in the back. My father was on a roll.

One day Naartjie was walking along the Berg River. The Boland sun beat down on his head, so he knelt to drink from the Blougat pool. As he reached out his hand to scoop up water, he saw a beautiful face in the water, beautiful beyond the magic of words or songs to capture it. Whenever he kissed the waterlips, the face melted. And so Naartjie stayed on the banks of the Berg River, staring into the water, pining away with longing for himself.

Then fishbubbles bubble up through my fingers and I turn to Moses:

– I found it.

He peers into the drum, and smiles:

– Good.

He makes me feel skilled, as if I landed a fish instead of just finding a hole in a tube.

At the crossroads down the street a bakkie revs, and jumps red. Tyres claw for grip as the gas kicks in. The pedal is flat and the bakkie shoots by full tilt, one man up front and two on the back. One of the backriders holds a shotgun high in one hand. Although you sometimes see an army lorry rumble through the streets, with soldier guns cocked at the sky, it is an uncommon thing to see a man out of uniform ride around with a gun.

– They are the boys, Moses says to me, the two on the back.

Further up the road, there is a jamming of rubber as the bakkie U-turns, and heads back. It gears down and skids to a halt in front of the diesel pump.

Moses switches off the radio.

The man behind the wheel has a tattoo in the bare skin of his head. He hoots the horn and calls out:

– Hey, Jimboy. Fill up with arabjuice.

Moses reaches for the hose. The numbers of the pump blink back to zero like the wide eyes of a scared comicbook character.

– Tell them you want your pass, I whisper into Moses' ear.

– Douglas, they are hard boys.

– Hey, you guys have stolen this man's pass, I yell at them.

– Well, check this out, old Jimboy found himself an albino monkey, says the shotgun cowboy on the back.

– Leave the boy alone, says Moses, his hand quivering on my head.

– What pass? the tattooed head wants to know.

– Forget it, Pa. This blek is fulla shit.

The other boy on the back, with the baboon-ass ears of a

rugby prop, laughs a high-pitched laugh. The sort of laugh that, in a comic, would be written: tee hee hee hee.

Moses shakes his head.

– Baas, the boy is right. They took my jacket with my pass in the pocket.

The shotgun cowboy and the rugby prop jump down from the back, as if on signal.

– You got something to say, old kaffir? demands the shotgun cowboy.

– Ya, you got something to say? goes the rugby prop.

– I want no trouble. I just want my pass.

– Oooh, shame. Old Jimboy lost his dog licence, says the shotgun cowboy to the tattoo-headed father behind the wheel.

– Sad story, tuts the tattooed head. But you are going too far, accusing my boys of stealing your jacket.

– But they did steal it and now the post office will not give him his money, I blurt out.

– Hey, Jimboy, where you find this monkey? jibes the shotgun cowboy.

– He is a good boy, baas.

– Now you be a good boy too, Jim, and make no trouble in this town, or you'll be sorry, goes the shotgun cowboy as he turns to look down the road.

Then he spins around and stabs Moses in the stomach with the barrel of the gun.

My heart beats wildly and I want to run. Moses holds his stomach, as if to catch his guts.

– What shall I stir up, baas? I just want my papers, Moses mouths under cast-down eyes.

– Well, the truth is, Jim, you bleks hate your pass. So we did you a favour and cut it up.

– That was a cruel thing to do, baas.

The shotgun cowboy yanks his knee up against Moses' balls. Moses slumps to the tar, with a long low moan, the moan of a shot Christmas cow on Oom Jan's farm. They tow Moses by his feet, round to the back of the garage. His head jigs on the tar, trailing a spoor of liquid, like snail slime.

– We got nothing against you, boy, but if bleks are free to run around telling stories, this country will go to pot, tunes the shotgun cowboy.

A Volkswagen kombi drives by the garage with a Neil Young tune sailing out of the windows. The man at the wheel is wearing ski shades with leather on the sides like donkey blinkers. He does not see us. I pick up the words: *I been to Hollywood, I been to Redwood, I crossed the ocean for a heart of gold.* The words fade as the kombi goes.

Moses is down under the beach umbrella that shades the doorstep of his room. The shotgun cowboy is booting him in the ribs.

– Don't you get white with us, Jimboy.

He kicks again. Moses rolls on the tar. In my head the needle sticks in a groove and all I think is: Please God, don't let him die. Please God. Please God. Then the needle jumps and I think: They'll kill me too. I survived sharks and baboons to be skopped to death. My ribs will cave in and then I will sink into the place of shadows and reflections.

I jika on my heels and begin to run.

– You run to the police, the shotgun cowboy barks after me, and we keel the old man.

I falter, sway on my heels. My mind mists.

I hear Neil Young over the deep chugging of a Volkswagen motor: *I been a miner for a heart of gold.* The kombi has turned around.

Hope sweeps the mist out of my mind.

– Let him go, I yell.

– Kom, julle, calls the father to his sons.

I hear the dull thud of the cowboy's boots landing in Moses' stomach, but Moses makes no sound.

Please God, I cry out inside my head.

As they go, I hear the rugby prop:

– Did you kick him dead?

– You crazy. You can't kick a kaffir dead. You have to pump a bullet in the head.

Behind me, the Isuzu bakkie kicks into life.

I drop to my knees and put my ear to his mouth. Through the *chook chook* chugging of the Volkswagen and the voice of Neil Young, I can just hear his breath: the sigh of a wind off the vlei. The motor chokes out. Overhead, the tassles of the beach umbrella dance and the strung shells jingle in the breeze. I hear a hoot for petrol. But Moses lies still, with his knees tucked in, like a dog by a fire.

I run around the corner. The man in the ski shades is standing by his kombi. I go up to him and grab his hand, wordlessly.

– What the hell? he cries, tipping his shades up onto his forehead.

Maybe it is the horror in my eyes that makes him follow me around to where Moses hugs his knees, a bleeding old-man foetus.

When he sees Moses, the kombi man just goes:

– Jesus Jesus Jesus Jesus

He is unaware of the river of words. He runs back for the water-can you use to fill a radiator and pours water over Moses' head. Moses splutters, then wipes his fingers over his eyes and nose and mouth, the way coloured kids do on Oom Jan's farm when they come up from under the dam water.

– Are you alright? the kombi man wants to know.

– Ndilungile, baas. This old kaffir, he does not die so fast.

– Some guys in a bakkie beat him up, I chip in.

– We better get the police, says the kombi man.

– Please, no police. I have no pass. The police will send me back to the Transkei.

– But we have to do something.

– There is nothing to do, baas.

The kombi man reaches out his hand to hoist Moses to his feet.

I open the door to Moses' room and fetch cold tap water in his enamel cup.

– Ndiyabonga, young baas.

He winces when he swallows.

I know it is because there is another white man there that he calls me baas. But I want him to call me Douglas. I want him to hold me and forgive me. But a black man does not hold a white boy.

– Jesus, at times I am ashamed to be white, says the kombi man.

He shakes his head.

– Well, I gotta hit the road. Gotta make Jo'burg tonight. I was running low on petrol, so I turned around. But I'll go to the BP up the road. You take it easy.

– No, baas. I am the petrolboy. If I am too weak to pour petrol then they must come and shoot me.

He hobbles towards the pumps, dragging one foot and hugging his ribs.

⁂

I stand on the bridge, listening for the sound of the diesel motor, but it is hard with the seagulls cawing for bread. But then I hear it. I wait till the sound changes under the bridge and then drop the brick. It falls and I think I have dropped it too soon, but no, the front of the Isuzu shoots into view and the brick floats through the glass. The bakkie swerves and flips. The shotgun cowboy is flung from the back. The bakkie careers into a roadside ditch. The cowboy lies dead in the dust and the crows flock to peck his eyes. I hear the sound of their beaks dipping into the jelly of his eyes. I can hear from so far. I see the beaks dip dip dip and come up red. My eye is a zoom lens.

I scream into my mother's nightie. She holds me to her breasts, the way she did then, till the screaming fades to a sobbing and the story of Moses and his papers and the Isuzu boys tumbles out.

popping frogs

I cycle alone out of town on the north road, the road to Johannesburg. I am determined to find a skeleton or something for Marika, but all I see are Simba packets hooked on the barbed wire and rusting tins of Coca-Cola and beer, and a red shotgun cartridge faded pink by the sun. It has not rained in two years and the earth is bone dry.

I see a lizard scurry into a Coca-Cola can.

A jacky hangman on the telegraph wires watches me watching it.

Although I am on the other side of the yellow line, riding on the jagged edge of the tar, a bus hoots at me and I feel the tug of wind in the wake of it. A stamp-sized square of paper butterflies up in the wind and settles again. I drop my bicycle to pick it up. Just paper. I flick it over in my fingers and see that it is not just paper, but part of a faded photograph of a black man. An ear, an eye, a cheekbone, a jagged edge where the nose should be. I stare at the photograph while something tickles my mind, a memory of some kind. Then it dawns on me that this could be Moses, younger and faded.

The Kodak photographs from the spool I saved from the baboons lie scattered on the kitchen table. My mother has not shot off another spool since we came to the Karoo. Why she has had them developed now, after so long, is a mystery to me.

The first photograph that catches my eye is of my father braaiing on a vine-stump fire, his lips snarled back to reveal his teeth. He stabs at the lens with the fire tongs as if he is a Zulu warrior with an assegai. There is fire in his eyes. Behind him, on the grid, slit crayfish cook in their shells.

I flick through photographs of the coral tree in bloom.

Then there is one of Marsden, standing beside his surfboard. He has unzipped his Zero wetsuit and the arms dangle like fins from his hips. I feel a pang of regret, for all the times I felt it unfair he should be so damn good at surfing and drawing.

There is a shot of Byron in the yard, his foot resting on the lug of a spade while he rolls a cigarette out of newspaper and Boxer tobacco. In the background Chaka burrows under the hibiscus.

There is a photograph of my mother in black bra and panties. She reaches out to the camera, as if to block the lens, but all she does is obscure her face. I know it is my mother because of the pink delta lines on her stomach from Marsden and me. The flash makes her skin look waxy.

There is one of me on the stoep, rubbing linseed into the Gunn & Moore bat. Though he is not in the photograph, I know that my father is just out of frame, reading the *Cape Times*, calling out the cricket scores, wondering if he ever told us that he once bowled out Barry Richards.

There is a shot of my father caught unawares at his typewriter.

The postcard of the Venus de Milo, tacked to the wall, curls up at the edges. In his eyes there is a guilty, fugitive look. The look I see in Chaka's eyes when I catch him shitting in the yard.

Then there is an out-of-focus shot of all four of us on the terrace of The Brass Bell, on the edge of the sea. My father has his arm around my mother, but he is not looking at her, or at the camera. He casts his gaze somewhere out to sea. Towards a yacht on the horizon, or Seal Island, or begging seagulls. For the first time, I wonder if my father was still in love with my mother when Marsden died. I imagined that the cricket ball splintered their love, as it did the tomato-box wicket. But what if their love was already falling apart and he longed to sail away from all of us to write his novel? To sail out to sea alone, like old man Santiago, to land the big fish he senses is out there.

Marika dances barefoot on the N1 in her cotton dress and tastes the falling rain with a lolling tongue. Skyfire flickers across a dark sky. For me the rain is not something magic, but Marika is over the moon, dancing, slapping her feet down on the tar.

After the rain the desert floats in a green, fishtank light. A river of frogs hazards the N1. Some make it across. Others pop under the singing wheels of motorcars, pink insides squirting out their mouths. Marika fills buckets of frogs and I cart them across the road and spill them out on the other side. She catches them with her bare hands and laughs at my fear of touching the cold, pulsing things.

As I weave through the flat frogs on the tar, swinging a squirming witchbrew of frogskin, I pray that they will not jump and brush against my hand, or land on my sandalled feet. When I spill them out I stand back, as a frog's compass may spin haywire and send the frog hopping back towards me, instead of following the eastward drift of the others. They stay in a dazed, blinking-eyed clutch, until Chaka's sniffing nose spurs them on again. They all head east.

pink poppies

Marika tugs her dress over her head and hangs it in the thorny mimosa. Then she lies down on the sand in her panties, floating flamingo-pink poppy nipples on koppies of unsunned skin. I yearn to lick her poppies.

— I want to feel the sun on my skin before I dive in, she says.

I lie down beside her, just in my underpants. Under my spine the sand burns. I turn my head, shut one eye against the sun and squint through the other at Marika. An ant comes over the horizon of Marika's hip. Its feelers quiver as it finds its bearings. Then it heads out along the bony curve of her hip. When it reaches the flat of her stomach it zeroes in on her bellybutton. It halts on the rim, feelers twitching. I shut both eyes and her poppies spin into swirling colour fans behind my eyelids.

Chaka's bark jolts me out of my sunflared dream. I squint against the sun and make out the eyes of a twin-barrelled shotgun fixed on me.

— Pa, Marika cries. Don't shoot him.

Rows of desks like conjugated Latin verbs. Mister McEwan reads the *Rime of the Ancient Mariner* to us. His reading is lost on me because my mind drifts:

Marika's father at our frontyard gate, his fingers noosed around Marika's neck.

– They are still children, Meneer Vink. It does not mean anything, my mother said.

– I am not having my daughter running wild with your boy and turning into a whore girl.

He yanked Marika after him. Her free hand dangled lifelessly, like the hand of a puppet when the string goes slack. He kicked at the door and Marika's ghost mother drew them into the dark of the house.

⌒

Because my head is full of Marika's pink poppy nipples my mind is not on my schoolwork. Teachers are after me to focus in class. They stab at my foolscap with red pens. Meneer van Taak barks at me to learn my sin, cos and tan. Mister McEwan kills the fly of a *comma* after the *s*, when it should come before, as if it is a sin. As if I care.

I have to work out the value of the angle Y in a spiderweb of pencilled lines before the cane comes down on my head.

Y is a fork in a river.

Wye is a river.

Y is a fish tail.

Y is a tale with two endings.

Y is a cattie for potting birds off a wire.

Y is the peace sign my father gives in the photograph where he looks like Cat Stevens on the back cover of *Tea for the Tillerman*.

Y is the taboo junction of leg under Miss Forster's skirt.

My father, Jack Daniel's happy, tells Marsden and me he saw a snake in a bar in Bangkok slither into a woman's Y, U-turn and come out again. Not to tell mother, he says.

A snake: two eyes in one ending of y-less tube.

It was on the wireless on Boxing Day.

Something catches my eye. A glint in the sand. A coin? No. A tiddly bit of glass peering out of the sand. I unbury a jam jar. Bottled in the foggy glass are a lizard and a snake. The lizard has shed its tail. The snake's Y-tongue flickers red. I untwist the lid, but neither moves. I fish the lizard out with a splinter of driftwood, as if it is a pickled gherkin. It looks dead but its ribs pulse as it sucks in the air. Then, with a flick of tail, it is gone into a black crab crack in the rocks. The dazed, flickery-tongued snake I bottle again and bury in the sand.

– Focus, bellows Van Taak.

The sting of the cane flares across my scalp. My fingers burrow under my hair to see if the skin is split. I will go bald before I get the hang of maths.

The woodwork teacher, Meneer Akkers, who is doddery and half-blind, canes me for my dovetail joints. He holds the joint up to the light and peers at it through his wine-bottle lenses. Light slivers through where the wood does not fit snugly. Because of his poor eyes, his cane does not land squarely on my ass, but cuts under.

When I undress for PT, I am ashamed of the red welts peeping out of the hem of my Speedo. I wish I could wear surfing baggies down to my knees, but Meneer Bester has banned baggies. Moffies wear baggies with flowers and shit on, he reckons. So the Klipdorp boys swim in their black Speedos.

Joost stands by the pool with an assegai of a bone in his Speedo. Instead of hiding it with his hands, he flaunts it, until Meneer Bester's eyes zoom in on his bone, under a taut tent of Speedo. Meneer Bester makes Joost do push-ups by the side of the pool. He grinds his Nikes into Joost's spine as if stubbing out a cigarette. He flicks factor 15 warpaint across his cheeks and stands there like a photographed hunter over his kill. Joost begins to quiver like a beaten, cowering dog, but Meneer Bester makes him go on until he bawls.

⌒

My mother is after me to be home for tea before dark. Not to drink milk from the carton like a backveld boy. To fetch bones from the butcher for Chaka, and to monkey through his hair for ticks, as Karoo ticks kill dogs. To rub away the shit Hope's chickens drop on Indlovu's roof. To rescue the chickens out of Chaka's gob when he chases them. Not to hang around at the Shell drinking Coca-Cola.

So my life goes. I am forever being plucked out of my day-dreams by cane-swinging teachers and my mother-hen mother.

walkabout

Now Chaka has gone walkabout. My mother reckons it is because he can smell a bitch out there somewhere. Hope reckons he is on his way back down the N1 to Cape Town.

When the afternoon school bell goes, I cycle down Delarey, keeping an eye peeled for Chaka. I swing in at the Shell, but Moses has not seen Chaka.

I reach the far edge of town, where there is a bus stop for the township taxis and buses.

The bus stop is a makeshift market, with fruit piled up on grass mats, and raw meat stacked on planks on top of 40-gallon drums, out of reach of the bony, tatty-eared dogs that shoo flies away from their eyes with a flick of the head.

I rest here, on the edge, to watch the haggling. Bob Marley's voice comes sailing out of a boombox. Meat is being braaied on a big fire. The meat catches fire, and a man, who turns it with his bare fingers, dips the burning meat in a bucket of water and then throws it on the fire again. The smoke of the fire mingles with the smoke pumped out of buses and hangs in a haze over the market.

A man, hobbling on his knees, bounces a football on his head. Sometimes a coin lands in his hat.

There is a billboard for Tiger Balm, and another for Omo washing powder.

A caravan has been turned into a cobbler's shop. A rastaman bobs his dreads to the Bob Marley beat as he knifes out a worn-down sole. Above the window stand the words: Ja Shoe Fix.

A barber shaves a man's scalp bald under a bare tree. His razor is wired to a motorcar battery, as if he wants to jump-start his head. A mirror dangles from a nail in the bark. OK Bazaars and Pep Stores bags hooked up in the tree bend it like ripe fruit.

Two old men sit smoking long pipes on a red motorcar seat under the shade of a black umbrella. They survey the chaos before them with a calm dignity, as if they have a box in the Baxter Theatre.

I catch sight of Chaka begging from a man who is gnawing at a chicken foot. I call to Chaka, but Chaka does not hear me. The man boards a bus and Chaka follows him up the steps. As I run across the market place the bus moves off, and the chicken foot flies out the window. I catch up with the bus and fist against the door. The driver waves me away, as if flicking flies from his face. As I drop back, faces look down from open windows at me.

– Baleka baleka! Run run, some cry.

– Hamba! Go away, others cry.

A ladder runs up to the roof rack. I reach out for it. It feels as if my bones will jerk out of joint, but I hold on and swing my feet up onto the bottom rung. Beside my head is the back window that can be kicked out if the bus crashes. Faces squash up against it like gaping fish. I wonder why they do not tell the driver. The bus tries to buck me from the ladder as it hits the ribbed dirt road. Jolts run up my shins and up my spine, and I have to clench my gibbering teeth. Dust smokes up into my face, and when I turn to the window faces again, I feel my eyeballs scratch inside the sockets. I squeeze my eyes shut against the dust and cling on.

After a time, the bus grinds to a halt. I open my eyes to see that we are in the township of shacks and broken cars and pyramids of rubble and plastic bags fluttering on barbed wire.

Girls with baby brothers or sisters bound in blankets on their backs fill jerrycans and drums with water at a tap.

There is a shop with an ad for BB tobacco on the zinc roof. The roof is anchored by rocks against gusts. Below the roof, in the shade of the stoep, a pack of skinny boys chatter in Xhosa. Behind them, the words *Nobody makes better tea than you* and *Five Roses*. They listlessly throw pebbles at me, perhaps to see if I am alive as I hang on the ladder, covered in dust like clay-painted abakwetha.

– Hey, I shout.

I jump and they scatter. When I just stand there, they regather, stones in hand, just in case. Then Chaka runs up and does his spinning bobtail war dance. They scatter again, until they see he is after his own tail and not their heels. They giggle at the sight, and home in again.

– What is your name? say lips under a faded Chicago Bulls cap.

– Douglas.

– What do you want in this place?

– I want my dog.

Chaka has given up his war dance to lick the dust off my knees, but his stump of a tail still wags.

– Your inja has found you, says a boy with spiky hair.

– Yes, he has found me.

– What is the name of your dog? the boy in the Bulls cap wants to know.

– Chaka.

The Xhosa boys fall about laughing. They think it is fitting that the name of a Zulu king be given to a dog.

– How will you go back to town? comes from the Bulls cap.

– I don't know. I have no imali for a ticket.

– We will walk with you. It is only five miles. But first, we do the township tour.

I follow the pack of barefoot boys down an alley between shanty shacks. A sweet smell hangs in the air. The boys suck their fingers and roll their eyes, so I figure it is dagga. They take me to a shack with a wood door. The bottom half of the door is pad-locked, and the top is ajar.

– Jonga, jonga, they cry.

So I look, peering into the dark. A smell of pee mingled with rotting fruit, but I see nothing. As I turn away, some snaky thing darts out of the dark and latches onto my arm. It is a sinewy hand with long yellowed nails. I yell and writhe, but the nails dig deeper into my skin. Chaka goes berserk and jumps up to bite the hand. For a while he hangs by his teeth and then drops again when the boys stone him. I see drops of red where Chaka's teeth punched through the skin. But still the hand holds me.

A face looms out of the gloom. A wild-eyed man with matted hair. He yips like a hyena at the sight of his dusty catch. I think he is going to drag me into the dark and eat me. Behind me I hear the boys giggling. Maybe they have fed white boys to the hyenaman before. The boy in the Bulls cap peels a banana and the man's eyes swivel across to the fruit. The boy holds the peeled banana out and the hyenaman lets go of my hand and snatches the fruit. I fly backwards. The man shrinks into the shadows, and the last thing I see is half the banana hanging from his lips like a long white tongue.

Chaka licks my face and the boys reel with laughter as if they have drunk a drum of marula juice or something.

I turn and run. With Chaka at my heels, I wind my way through the riddle of paths that tunnel through eyeless tumble-down shacks.

– Baleka baleka! Run run, a girl calls from a shadowy doorway.

This spurs me on. I jump abandoned tyres and cracked jerry-cans and potholes. Then I see the girl again, clapping her hands with glee at the sight of a white boy and his dog boomeranging back past her door.

I am lost. I falter to a halt and stoop to free a stone from my sandals. Chaka licks my face with a hot panting tongue. But I jackinthebox up again when a voice calls after me:

– Hey boy! Wait for us.

I run on, imagining they have another game in mind. I fling myself around corners, dodging chickens and a woman carrying a cardboard box on her head.

– Tixo, she cries as I run by and her hands shoot up to steady the tilting box.

I run past a man in a black Che beret and Biggles goggles doing karate at the slow, studied pace of a climbing chameleon.

I reckon I have lost them, when I spin around a corner and see them ahead of me. My heart pounds. There they stand, fingers peeking out of torn pockets. The boy in the Bulls cap whistles a birdcall, and somewhere behind me I hear an echo. I know they have me cornered. I finger the seeds in my pocket and glance around for an escape. I catch sight of Marsden reflected in a blind paraffin-tin window.

– Hey, it was just a joke, the boy in the Bulls cap calls across the gap. All he wants is a banana.

He comes towards me, followed by the shadow of another boy.

– My name is Joko, and this is Lucky.

Lucky, his spiky-headed shadow, nods his head and hitches up his shorts. They are a man's shorts and have to be folded a few times to hook on his bony hips.

– Ndiyakubona, goes Lucky.

– I see you too, I go.

– And I am Tomorrow, pipes up a shorter boy with a mopani worm of snot peeping out of his nostril.

Joko glares at him. Tomorrow sniffs the mopani up into its hole again, and drops into the background of unnamed boys.

My fear ebbs. It is hard to be scared of boys called Tomorrow and Lucky.

– Come and have a drink, says Joko.

– Ya, come on, says Lucky.

– Okay.

We go past an outdoor school where only the teacher sits in a desk, surrounded by children. She looks comical, a big fat woman squeezed into a small school desk. She does not smile as the boys go by and nod at her. Her voice does not miss a beat:

– Swim swam swum, goes the teacher sandwiched into the desk.

– Swimswamswum, the children chant.

I wonder where they can swim in a bone-dry township so far west of the Zeekoe River, and hundreds of miles from the sea.

We go inside a dark shack. There is a table covered with a plastic cloth with faded London landmarks on it. Joko pulls up a rickety bentwood chair for me. He and Lucky sit on upturned Coca-Cola crates. Tomorrow and the small boys sit on the floor.

– I've been to London, I say.

– Did you drink tea with the queen? says Lucky.

– No.

– Why go all the way to London and not see the queen?

– Well, she lives behind high walls with her dogs.

– Dogs, Tomorrow echoes and sniffs his snot up again. You can tell it makes an impression on him that the queen has dogs.

– Is she also scared, like the whites in Jo'burg, with their dogs and high walls? Joko wants to know.

– No, there is nothing to be scared of in London, because no one is hungry. If you have no job the government gives you money, they call it the dole. There are beggars, but my father says they beg because they have dopped their dole away, or because they know they can trick the tourists.

– The government just give you the money?

– Ya.

– Even if you are black, they give you the money?

– Ya.

– Jesus. I tell you man, I'm going to London. Hello, Madam Queen.

He makes a bow and the others laugh.

– Did you see Liverpool play? Tomorrow wants to know.

– No, I never went to a football game.

You can tell they think I am crazy.

There are chipped glasses on the table. Joko pours Stoney ginger beer from a litre bottle and, when it runs dry, twists open a bottle of Coca-Cola. I get to choose first, and I go for the Coca-Cola. It is lukewarm. I wonder if they have ever had Coca-Cola with ice and a slice of lemon, or a Coke float.

When I put my glass down, Joko says:

– It is time to go.

I follow Joko and Tomorrow and Lucky and the boys, Chaka at my heels. In the distance we see the orange haze of a veld fire. We stand on the verge of the road, this side of the barbed wire of a farm border, and watch the black farmboys fighting the flickering flames, flinging down long sticks with rubber flippers wired to the ends. The fire has burnt from the tar road across a farm towards the distant koppies, a black sea under the moon.

Then we hear a sound smoke out of a nearby ditch and run up to it to find a black man lying beside a bicycle. Runnels of blood follow the furrows of his forehead. The whites of his scared eyes are bloodshot. Xhosa words spill from his mouth, a scattering out of clinking bones and shells. My dodgy Xhosa is not up to disentangling the words.

It turns out, Joko tells in a bitter voice, that the man, called Zeph, was cycling along when he saw a fire in the veld. He got off his bike. Just then a farmer came up in his bakkie and accused Zeph of flicking a match into the grass. No, baas, it was not me, went Zeph. He had once done a stint of sheep dipping for the farmer, Baas Aalfänger. Surely the baas would remember him, that he was a good worker. But Baas Aalfänger did not recall an individual black face. Instead he bade Zeph empty his pockets. Unfortunately for Zeph, he had a Bic lighter in his pocket. Aalfänger needed no more proof. He got a spade from the back of the bakkie and swung it at Zeph's head. Then he broke his shins with the spade and left Zeph in the ditch for the jackals.

– We have to get him to a doctor.

– No, we will look after him. If he goes to town the farmer will have him jailed. It is his word against a white man's.

Joko spits the words at me, as if blaming me. Then he turns to Tomorrow and tunes them something in Xhosa. Joko holds his head, and each of them goes for a foot or a hand.

Tomorrow picks up the bicycle. It is a black, fat-tyred, township bicycle, like the omafiets bicycles I saw in Amsterdam. They hoist him up on to the bicycle and prop him up with their arms. His head lolls as they wheel him along the edge of the tar, back towards the township.

— Goodbye, I call after them.

— Bye, calls Joko.

But he does not turn his head. At this moment I am just another white skin to him. Only spiky Lucky glances back at me. One hand hangs on to his shorts to keep them from falling off his hips. The other helps to steady the injured Zeph. No hand free to wave.

I begin to run. Chaka lopes beside me, tongue sliding across his grinning teeth.

masai cocktail

A shot bangs through the afternoon haze. Then another. Moses and I run from the junkyard, where the Volvo perches on bricks, bleeding black oil into a Koffiehuis tin.

As we round the corner a hissing tomcat darts by with its hair spiked up along the spine. I see the yahoo brothers jump into their bakkie and Isuzu out onto the road, revs howling, tyres smoking. Across the road Ou Piet Olifant shakes a tablecloth at the Isuzu, as if to shoo evil away, then hobbles over towards us.

A yowling floods my ears. I follow Moses round to the back. In front of his room half a dozen cats writhe on the floor. My eyes zone in on the flipped milk tin, and the seeping of cat blood into milk. Blood sifts through the cat fur in random patterns.

Moses plucks up a ginger cat by its scruff. With his free hand he catches the slimy guts as they snake out. He holds the head of the cat to his collarbone. I hear a sound, like a distant lowing, well up in Moses. Then he lets the guts go. He hoods the cat's head with the blooded hand, and gives the head a twist, as if shutting a tap. Through the yowling of bleeding cats, I hear the bone snap.

He tosses the floppy-headed cat into the 40-gallon drum, among empty Castrol cans and rags stained with dipstick oil.

One by one, Moses holds the cats to his collarbone, so their fur lies against his cheek.

One cat, in the frenzy of dying, claws a tattoo into Moses' skin.

dead boer

Marika and I cycle north out of town, heading for Salem. She reckons her father will skin her if he catches her in the township. Still, she is keen to go. The sky is an endless blue canvas. A full moon hovers on the horizon, on the verge of ballooning into the blue sky.

North is the way to Johannesburg, through Bloemfontein, where Tolkien was born. Mister McEwan cannot understand how the mind that mapped out Middle Earth could have been born in such a barren, godforsaken place. For Mister McEwan, all the world south of England is godforsaken.

Marika rides along the yellow line instead of weaving across the road. I am not sure if it is the township ahead, or the full moon, casting a mood over her.

– It is a sign, Marika says of the moon. Like when it's sunny and it rains.

– A monkey's wedding?

– Ya, a monkey's wedding, nods Marika.

– What's it a sign of?

– A monkey's wedding?

– No, the moon under a blue sky.

– It is a sign of magic.

But no moon magic can change things back to the moment before my father bowled the ball, before my life was halved:

Marsden taps the foot of the bat in the sand. A sand yacht flits by. The fruitsellers call their wares. The sound of the seagulls spears through the hazy hiss of the surf, a sound that ebbs out of mind, and then surges back again. And then, high over the humming bass of motorcars, the ting ting ting *of the lollyboy's bell.*

We cycle past a donkey cart laden high with thorn wood. The donkey hide is raw pink where the ropes have chafed through.

Further along, a cow skull flowers out of the sand, but Marika hardly gives it a glance. Perhaps cows are not as exotic as lizards.

As we reach the outskirts of the township, a bus rumbles by. The wind sucks at us and voices fling from the windows. Then it is past and I see heads bob in the back window. I am glad I am not clinging to the roof-rack ladder.

On the outskirts of the township men play football on a sand pitch while women sway and whistle on the sides. The men have team shirts on, striped yellow and black, like bees. Some wear baggy PT shorts and some wear hacked-off jeans. Football socks of all colours concertina down bare shins. A ball flies into the net. A footballer cartwheels and the women dance and go *uluuu uluuu uluuu.*

There is no sign of Joko's Chicago Bulls cap among the crowd.

We cycle to the square where the bus stands empty outside the general dealer shop with the BB Tobacco sign on the roof.

Barefoot boys chase a flat, farting football in the dust. One of the boys is Tomorrow. I call out to him, and he glances my way before darting down an alleyway. I picture Tomorrow sniffing up his mopani snot as he reports to Joko that the white boy is back.

Again, girls fill jerrycans at the tap, their bare toes sunk deep in mud.

An old man sits in the sun, flies sipping the liquid in the corner of his eyes.

Tinny Soweto jazz floats out of the dark of the shop into the afternoon glare, mingles with the Xhosa clicks of the girls and the clowning of the boys.

– Would you keep an eye on our bikes? I say to the old man.

He nods his head and the flies scatter like spat pips before zoning in on his eyes again.

We lean our bikes against the wall of the shop. I hear the *ping* of pinball and peek into the dark to see if Joko and the boys are hanging out in the shop. My eyes slowly focus: a lone man is pinballing. He lets go the flipper buttons to take a swig from a bottle of Black Label, but his darting eyes still follow the zigzag path of the ball. He clunks the bottle down onto the glass deck just in time to flip the ball with a flick of his hips.

The shopkeeper is on a ladder, counting cans of tuna and Koo fruit, notching pencil marks on paper. Seeing me, he pockets the paper, fits the pencil stub behind his ear. He comes down the ladder slowly, like a wise old man with the secrets of a myriad lost books in his head.

– May I help you?

– I was looking for Joko.

– It is better you go home. This is no place for white boys.

– But I know him.

– Go now, young baas.

The pinball man, beer bottle in hand, weaves towards me.

– Hey, you. You hamba home now. Your white skin is a reminder of our shame. When we see you in town, it is another thing. There we bow, we bend, we beg, knowing at the end of the day we can hamba home to our tin and zinc pondoks, drink our beer, hear our fever music and forget. When you come here, you rub the shame in our face, remind us we are cowering dogs. You think you know Joko, but you know shit.

    – Let him go, pleads the shopkeeper. He's still a boy. The world is not of his making.

    – You know shit, spits the pinballer.

    He sways out into the afternoon glare.

    – It's Saturday afternoon, says the shopkeeper. The same man, Monday to Friday, is the delivery boy for Smuts, the chemist. You know Smuts?

    I nod, but hear the pinballer's echo in my head: you know shit.

⌒

Marika follows me into the jigsaw of cluttered shanties. The narrow paths do not have street names, but numbers graffiti the doors.

    Whenever we come to a junction, I choose a path, randomly. Marika follows, unaware that I have lost my bearings. I want to be heroic in her eyes, navigating through the maze of shanties.

    We go past a window in which a pig's head hangs on a hook. Flies buzz around the gaping mouth. I wonder if Chaka would have ended up hanging from a hook if I had not found him. Blacks love pig head and chicken feet, but maybe it is just the Chinese who chow dog.

    I walk on. After a while I see the fly-hassled, hooked pig's head again. Fortunately, Marika catches sight of a stray orange cat, like the fat rabbit of a cat on the cover of *Teaser and the Firecat*, and she does not cotton on that I am lost. I try to fix my bearings by the sun over the flat zinc roofs.

Then, as if a theatre backdrop is whisked away, Joko and the boys are in front of me.

– Hi, Douglas, says Joko, reaching out his hand.

His palm is a flash of yellow ivory.

– Hi, Joko. This is my friend, Marika.

Marika looks up from scratching the firecat on its head.

– Hello, she says.

She offers Joko the firecat. Joko, puzzled, holds the cat.

– Come, says Joko, we have something to show you.

Joko drops the cat. It twists midair and lands on its feet. Unruffled, it begins licking its paws.

Marika and I follow Joko and the boys deeper into the maze. After a while we come to a clearing where rowdy men cluster like boys around a schoolyard fight. Joko bids us to go down on our knees. We peep through the legs of the men to see a baboon fighting a dog. The dog, a bull terrier, looks like an albino shark. He has the baboon's leg in his jaw and doggedly clings on as the baboon scratches at his cold, sharky eyes. The baboon's bone juts through the skin and the men are yelling and the baboon is going *chiii chiii chiii* and the dog makes a funny deep warbling sound.

Then the baboon rips the dog's ear off and blood flicks onto my face and Marika's dress. Marika cries out and runs.

The men spin around. Seeing me, big-eyed and blood-specked, they laugh, then swing back to the kill.

I run after Marika. Joko and the boys run after me. When we reach the square, Marika stops dead in her tracks. The bus is gone. Instead, her father stands there on the running-board of his Studebaker, facing the general dealer, waving his shotgun at the BB Tobacco sign, yelling:

– Come out, you bloody kaffirboetie. Where is my girl?

The pinballer is sitting on the veranda, his head lolling. The shopkeeper comes out with his hands up. It is a scene shot in a Mexican border town.

Through her tears, Marika begs:

– Douglas, hide. If he sees you he'll kill you.

We hide behind the carcass of a burnt-out Volkswagen taxi van. Over the thudding of my heart I hear a surging sound. For a moment I think it is the throbbing of blood in my head, but then I hear voices and my blood runs cold.

Dancers, spearheading the crowd, come into sight on the right. The drumming feet halt dead at the sight of the white man toting a gun, one foot on the running-board of his Studebaker. Chanting, happy-go-lucky heads shunt up behind the front row of stonewalled dancers. The chanting ebbs and laughter at the sight of the lone boer rivers through the crowd.

– Bly weg. Stay back, Marika's father yells, jabbing his gun at them.

Again there is a scattering of laughter at the man.

– Bly weg van my, he shrieks.

His voice frays with fear.

Marika's father shoots a cartridge into the sky. The shot bangs in my eardrums, then pinballs among the tin shacks.

For a moment it is still, and all I hear is the faint Soweto jazz drifting out from under the BB sign, and the cicada singing of the gunshot in my ears. It is a loaded, strung-out moment, like the freeze at the end of *Butch Cassidy and the Sundance Kid.*

A young man in a football shirt picks up a stone and listlessly lobs it at the Studebaker. The stone clatters on the roof of the motorcar.

In my head the Muizenberg monkeynut widow yells: Joo got no respect for the neighbourhood.

The barrel of the shotgun fires and a fat woman flops down.

Her black turban flips off and rolls in the dust. It holds the shape of her head, like a memory, until it is stomped underfoot. Yawning mouths bay for blood and fists jut into the pink, cowboy sky.

Marika's father jackknives the barrel. The red cartridge in his fumbling fingers will not go down the barrel. A stone lands on his bald head and blood petals away from the wound.

Marika lunges forward. I dive for her heels. The sand skims the skin off my elbows. I muzzle her mouth with my hand.

Marika's father rocks on his feet. The gun drops from his hands. Marika squirms under me, hissing-cat mad.

Marika's father flies into the sky, the tossed-up hero of the football game. For a moment, at the pivot of his flight, he floats. His eyes, brimful with fear, zoom into mine, and then the lust of yawning mouths sucks him down.

He stays down.

Joko and I drag Marika back behind the taxi van. I feel her heart pump against my ribs. I let her go. Her jaw gapes and out flies a scream that hurls me back to the beach, and my head in the hollow of my mother's breasts and the stench of burnt meat on Oom Jan's abandoned braai. Then the township shanties and the chanting fists rush back into focus. There are no beach umbrellas or fruitsellers or any signs of the familiar.

I clamp my hand hard over her mouth and she bites my finger through to the bone. I whisk my hand away and flick my fingers in a fevered air-guitar riff. Marika gulps down air. I fist her in the face. Blood runs into her mouth.

The Studebaker goes up in flames. Smoke inks the sky and figures jitterbug around the fire.

– You hamba out of here now, Joko calls.

I instinctively follow him, plucking Marika after me. The earth is wavy under my feet and the shanties dance. The din of the mob dims as we dodge through the alleyways, jink through the hazards of rubber tyres and dead bicycles. Marika's sobs mix with the *thup thup thup* of her footfalls on the hard earth. Then we reach the tar road.

– Forget the bicycles and baleka, says Joko.

The sun arcs low on the horizon. The earth loops round the sun. I have just seen a man murdered, yet the earth loops coolly on. It does not lurch or jolt when you die. It does not skip a beat, whether a cricket ball cracks your skull, or a randomly flung stone fans blood across your forehead.

My lungs burn. Marika runs behind me. Her sobbing has dried out. I fix my eyes on the yellow line on the tar ahead. I can't bear to turn and look into her unblinking, accusing eyes. I want to justify my fisting her in the face but the words wing away and I am too numb to catch at them. Words scatter like crow-pecked mossies and all that is left is this thudding of feet, the singing of the telegraph wires in the breeze, and the sickening lilt in the pit of my stomach.

Marika does not look back as she goes into their yard, and into the house where an unwitting widow waits in the dark.

I throw my shirt, stained with the blood of Marika and dog, in a dustbin that says: Hou die Kaap Skoon. Keep the Cape in Shape.

At the rainwater tank, I run my hands and elbows free of blood, hold my throbbing finger under the soothing flow. I climb through my window and pull on my father's University of Cape Town rugby jersey. I creep along the creaking floorboards to find my mother snoring at the kitchen table, her hand still holding a bottle of London Dry Gin. The red boar's head snarls his tusks at me.

Chaka awakes from his farting sleep and wags his stump. I go to my room with him and sit in the dark. Chaka laps the salt from my skin, licks my bleeding finger. My head is as hollow as the inside of Tennessee's gutted shell. I hear the roar of a Land Rover pulling up across the road. It did not take them long, as only one man drives a Studebaker in Klipdorp. Chaka growls and I tickle his ears to calm him. I gear myself for the scream, but it does not come. After a time, the Land Rover goes again.

☙

My head flies off the pillow. My heart pounds. My mind ferrets after the sound that woke me, frantic to catch it, defuse its horror by defining it, naming it. But all hint of the sound is gone, skoon out of my head. All I hear is the familiar ragged volley of Chaka's blunt barks, listlessly echoed by the other dogs of the neighbourhood.

The floorboards, cool under my bare feet, creak like a yacht mast in the wind. The zebra skin on the wall brushes against my skin. My mother stirs on the orange sofa in the front room. From the lip of a tipped glass, wine seeps into the floorboards. A candle on the window sill has burnt to a stub, oozing wax over the edge. The incense joss has gone out long ago, leaving a trail of fish-shit ash. Yet the smell of jasmine lingers, a wistful afterthought.

The kitchen door swings in the breeze, the moon glints off the lino. I sense that the sound came from out there, beyond the kitchen steps where Hope sits and peels sweet potatoes into her apron at dusk.

Hope's khaya is dark.

red rabbit

The death of Marika's father is reported on the front page of the *Daily Dispatch*. The headline, SOWETO HAS COME TO KLIPDORP, is a comment from Mevrou Pienaar, the café tannie at the Sonskyn Kafee.

The paper rumours that Marika's father, Willem Vink, may have been involved in illicit shebeen trading in Salem but Sergeant Verster, of the Klipdorp police, defends him: Ou Willem Vink was a deacon in the kerk. There is no way that he would stoop to such shady dealings.

Sergeant Verster goes on: I give you my word that no stone will be left unturned in our efforts to hunt down his killers.

My heart skips a beat. I wonder if I can be jailed for watching a murder. O Jesus, don't let Sergeant Verster find my bicycle and come after me.

Across the road the curtains stay drawn. I wonder if Marika is sad her father is dead even though he beat her and jerked off over the *Scope*.

☙

At school Marika's desk is empty. Meneer de Beer is writing on the blackboard. There are whispers that her father went to the township to fuck a kaffir girl.

– If I had a shotgun in Salem, I would shoot my way out, Clint Eastwood style, tunes Joost.

– We should have shot all the kaffirs long ago, jus' laaik the 'Mericans shot the Indians to hell 'n' gone, larks a wiry boy they call Biltong.

– Then there'd be no Soweto, or Salem, laughs Joost.

– And no gold, or roads, or Johannesburg, if you think of it, says Meneer de Beer.

The boys are rattled to find he has heard every word. They shift in their desks, ashamed.

Meneer de Beer hands out scalpels. We have to slit the foil to free the blades.

– Jus' laaik opening a rubber, jokes Joost, recovering his bravado.

Then Meneer de Beer tells us to pick a rabbit from the box.

Joost picks white.

– So the blood stands out, he chirps.

– Work in twos, commands Meneer de Beer. One to hold the rabbit down and one to slice through the windpipe.

Rabbits are yanked out of the box by their ears, feet clawing the air.

I am with a girl called Talia. She too has picked out a white rabbit, with red eyes. When Marsden and I were small, my mother would come into the room on the first of the month, saying: white rabbits, white rabbits. She has not done it for a long time. Not since my father said: you boys are becoming too old to waltz into the bathroom when your mother is naked.

Talia scratches the rabbit behind its ears.

– Wonder if he has a name? she says, to herself rather than me.

I can tell there is no way she is on the verge of slicing him open. So it is up to me, the boy. I have tugged heads off pigeons, seen blood squirt from a man's head and the bone of my finger peep through my skin. But, at the thought of slitting through the beautiful white fur, nausea waves through me.

I put up my hand.

– Douglas?

– I'm sorry, sir, but I won't cut the rabbit.

– What's that you said?

– I can't kill the rabbit.

– You can't kill an animal, yet you eat meat?

– I'm sorry, sir.

– Either you kill the rabbit, or you bend.

I hang my head.

– Look boy, I'm being cruel to be kind. In South Africa you don't have the freedom to be a moffie pacifist. Maybe overseas, where they don't care if you wear an earring or smoke dagga, but this is South Africa and we are at war. If you won't kill a rabbit at school, how will you kill a Cuban on the border? Hey? And if you don't pull the trigger, it's not just your life but the life of your fellow soldiers you risk.

– Moffie, I hear Joost whisper. You won't shoot but you'd suck McEwan's cock?

How Joost has jumped from rabbits to cock escapes me.

– Bend then.

Meneer de Beer swings down his cane.

– Now, will you kill the rabbit or shall I go on?

Though I feel sick and know that Marika would be ashamed of me, I pick up the scalpel.

I tilt the rabbit's head back by the ears, then slice into his windpipe. Blood seeps through his fur. His eyes glare and his hind legs jigger. I hold him down, until a shudder ripples under his skin and the lustre fades out of his eyes. Then I slit the stomach and the smoking guts slither out.

In Sea Point, the stitching on my amber-eyed, chewy-eared panda comes undone and the spongy stuffing tumbles out. My mother jams the sponge back in and sews it up again.

The classroom spins and I hear Talia scream across a misty beach before my head hits the sand.

Through flickering eyelids I see Meneer de Beer's eyeballs warping behind the lenses of his glasses. Red deltas in the whites of his eyes.

– You okay, Douglas?

I nod. He gives me a notched beaker of cold water.

After school, I walk along Delarey to the Shell.

Moses jumps up from his beer crate when he catches sight of me.

– I am happy to see you, Douglas. Marika's father was looking for you and there was fire in his eyes. He wanted to know where you had gone with his girl. I would not tell him. He cocked his shotgun. So I told him you had gone to Salem. I have been worried for you.

– He's dead.

– I heard it on the radio.

– I saw him die.

– Au au, Douglas.

– I'm glad he's dead.

– That is a hard thing to say.

– But how can you forgive a man who taught his daughter to hate blacks?

Moses stands there, wiping sump oil from his hands with a shammy.

– Maybe because he was a poor teacher, he smiles.

darting lizard

No barks to warn me. Marika's head is a silent half-moon floating at the window. My heart drums. I dare not move. Maybe it is just a phantom floating on the dark of my guilt. The one lit eye stares out of unbatting lids. There is no sign of feeling in it. She has come to cast a curse on me.

– Hey, Douglas, she whispers.

– I see you.

– My mother is sending me away, to boarding school in Pretoria.

– I'm sorry.

– Come out to the reservoir with me. To say totsiens.

– I thought you blamed me?

– Still, I want you to come.

I climb out of the window. Chaka, seagull-chaser, guineafowl-hunter, licks her legs for salt.

The town is sad and mute under a full moon. I chuck stones at Chaka to keep him from following us. A stone kicks up from the tar to nip his ribs. He yelps and slinks homewards in the tail-tucked way of tailed dogs.

– Let him be, Marika says.

But I don't want to share her, not even with a dog. When Chaka glances round to see if I feel sorry, I mimic another throw.

The Shell garage is deserted. I imagine Moses snoring on his bed, dreaming of the tokoloshe while the few surviving cats cruise the junkyard dark for rats.

The bell of the Dutch church chimes midnight.

It is a long walk to the reservoir but the night is magic: the stars blink like cats' eyes, and the crickets chorus. A bat swoops low, loops around us, and flits away. A porcupine rattles its quills at us.

⌒

We lie under the mimosa, where memory of the day's blazing sun lingers in the sand.

– I'm sorry you have to go.

– I will miss the horses, and the veld, and the reservoir.

My lip quivers as I squeeze back tears.

She sheds her dress.

– And I will never forget you.

She lies naked on the sand and tugs my head to her full, welling fruit and I suck it.

– It feels so beautiful, she purrs.

Under the mimosa under the moon I suck Marika's nipples raw.

She wriggles out from under me until my head lies between her thighs and her lovehair tickles my nose. My tongue is the unbottled lizard on Muizenberg beach, darting into fissured rock. Then it is just me, burrowing wordlessly into Marika as she sighs and rocks her hips on the warm sand.

I spurt into the sand. Damp for the downunder frogs.

jacaranda juju

In the convent in Pretoria, the nuns forbid Marika to wear short skirts. They have burnt her snakeskin. They have blacked out words from her letter to me.

I zippo a sandalwood joss, and finger the seeds of the coral as if they are rosary beads, in the hope of conjuring up images of Marika in exile. The sandalwood smoke drifts out into the dark, where crickets chirp and distant dogs bark in fits and starts. I wonder if you could write out such music of chance. How would random chirps and yips and yaps look in tadpole notes?

I armadillo into a ball on the orange sofa.

I see her in the place where long skirts hide her knees, scratched and scarred like the knees of a boy. She bends her head under a crucifix. Then she hikes her skirt up, and tucks it in so she can ladder down from a high window. I see her legs long and luminous in the moonshine. When her feet touch the grass, she peels her skirt away and weaves naked through the jacarandas. Jacaranda flowers pop under her feet and stain them indigo.

cowrie

While Mister McEwan reads Blake, I doodle a pencil house for Marika.

This is our house and this is Chaka. And this is the garden where Byron makes the flowers flower. Magnoliawisteriaoleander etcetera. And these are the kitchen steps where Hope peels potatoes in the sun. Come in.

This is the curtain I hid behind, the time my father wanted to beat me for calling Byron a nigger. Look at the motif of Chinese monks crossing arced bridges to an island of willows. Behind the willows fish heads and dead flowers kiss in a dustbin. See, up on the spice rack is a china dog. The dog eats milk chits. Each night Marsden and I fight over who is to put the chits out for the milkman. I call Marsden aasvoël to rile him and he calls me koggelmander. But you can tell he is sourpussed because I bagsed aasvoël first. After all, wouldn't you rather be a lizardy koggelmander than a bald bird with stinkbreath?

Through this door is where my mother and father sleep under

a fanblade. See, above my mother's pillow a crucifix hovers on the
wall like a dark, mothy insect.

And this is Marsden's room. See his seagull sketches tacked
to the wall, and this one of my mother's toes painted red. On the
sill, beside Tennessee the tortoise and jars full of porcupine quills
and paintbrushes, is something I forgot: a grass straw the Masai
punch through cow skin to suck hot blood. Beautiful, isn't it?
And, under the sill, a basket of tennis balls, and cricket balls with
unravelling seams, and a frisbee punctured by Chaka's teeth, and
juggling balls. Marsden, you see, is a juggler, and an artist. My
father says to Marsden: my boy, if you ever backpack through
the world you can survive by juggling on street corners. What
would I do to survive? Marsden reckons: Koggelmander, I juggle
and you gigolo.

Sometimes I slip into his bed at night, spines and footsoles
touching, turned away yet tuned in.

The hallway is rather bare, just a zebra skin on the wall. It
grazed yellow speargrass in Kenya, until my Grandpa's bullet
bit behind the ear. You can see where it is patched. I had never
thought of it, but you are right, it is undignified the way his legs
fan out flat, as if in flight. When I was a child I was so scared of the
buffalo head there, over the toilet door, that I rather peed out of
my bedroom window at night. Can you see the holes in his horns?
Like the holes woodworm bore into yellowwood kists.

Back in the classroom, so far from Cape Town where the sea
lilts to the mood of the moon, I wonder what happened to the
crucifix. Maybe it is buried in newspaper in an unpacked teabox.
Buried deep like the French book of black-and-white photographs
Marsden and I found on the promenade, in one of the blue bins.
Photographs of women with bare cowrieshell slits, or otherwise

hidden under fuzz, and nippleskin rippled like apples that begin to dry out. We hid the book in Marsden's sketch box. Then, fearing my mother would find it, we buried it under the pyramid of compost in the far corner of the backyard. Under weeds and orange rinds and potato peels and egg shells.

white doll

—Hand me the monkey, comes Moses' voice from under the Volvo.

I scratch in the toolbox for the monkey wrench. I love the long Sunday afternoons at the Shell with Moses. It is hard to believe it is four years since I pedalled by for Coca-Cola.

The Volvo glints yellow, no longer a hobo, but a funky convertible. Just her square eyes betray another life.

– Here is the monkey, Moses.

– Ndiyabonga, says Moses.

I know it makes Moses feel good when I call him Moses after another week of being Jimmed. Fill up with 97, Jim. Yes, baas. Oh, and do check the oil and water, Jim. Yes, madam. They do not know he has a brother dead down the mine and a brother gone north to Mozambique. They do not know he felt the sun on his face just one day a week for thirty years. For Moses South Africa was not braaivleis, rugby, sunny skies and Chevrolet, but pap and sour beer and football, and an endless maze of tunnels under the earth.

Moses comes up from under the Volvo.

– There, I fixed the diff. I just wish I could fix up the sadness in you. You cry for the girl gone to Pretoria.

He spits into his hands and rubs them.

– Pretoria. Sounds so pretty.

He gives a bitter laugh.

– Pretoria says you can work in Johannesburg. Pretoria says you must go back to the Transkei. Without the paper from Pretoria you are nothing. I have no hope now for a letter to come from Pretoria. Pretoria has no time for an old man who no longer goes down the mine. And now Pretoria wants your girl.

East of Klipdorp the sky colours red. A faraway rooster calls *yenkuku yenkuku* and Hope's chickens cluck restlessly.

I cycle through the dorp, heading for the Shell. As I turn into Delarey I hear the deep *rrum rrum* of the Volvo motor.

At the Shell, Moses says *molo* to me and shifts over to the other side. He is wary of driving without his papers. I get in behind the wheel. As we go, Chaka barks at the Volvo's tyres, until he drops away.

– One day we fuduka for good out of this Karoo, goes Moses.

– Fuduka, I echo. All the way to Cape Town.

I have one hand on the wheel, the other searches for a radio station. Radio 5 comes through clear as a record. Lou Reed walks on the wild side.

– And your cats, if we go?

– Ou Piet from the hotel will put out milk for them.

I tilt my head to suck in the cold wind that rapids over the windshield. On the dashboard Saint Christopher wades the monkey Jesus through the river.

Ahead a shepherd stands watching sheep graze the tall grass between the tar and the fenced grazing lands. From a distance he looks like a Masai with a long spear. Turns out it is just a long bamboo with a red handkerchief to flag cars. As we go by, he smiles pink gums at us.

Ahead a man waves in the street. Another shepherd? O Jesus, a roadblock. A policeman signals us to the side, where two other policemen gut the boot of a dented Datsun, while the coloured family cluster on the kerb. A little girl darts out from under her father's hand to pick up a kewpie doll from among the things on the kerb. The doll has a twist of plastic hair. The father tugs the girl back out of the way of the law.

We are close enough to hear the policemen, to see the doll's blue eyes.

– Kyk daar, jong, they so want to be white their kids play with white dolls, jokes the policeman with yellow arrows of rank on his greyblue uniform.

– Ja-nee, the unranked policeman shakes his head.

You would think the shadowless figures clustered under the zenith sun did not exist.

Through the murk of fear in my head, it dawns on me that I have never seen a black doll in a shop. Not in OK Bazaars or Spar, or any shop.

– No contraband goods. Jy kan ry, the father is told.

– Dankie, my baas, says the father, dipping his head.

He and his wife bend down to regather their scattered things.

Then the ranked policeman turns to me.

– Good day, sir. Your licence, please.

My heart drums a tattoo as I hand him my licence.

– Your licence is in order. Does the man beside you have a licence?

Moses keeps his eyes averted.

– A licence?

– A pass. A licence to be out of his homeland.

– All his papers were stolen, sir.

– Do you mean to say you have no pass for the Bantu?

Moses bows his head under the inevitable.

– His pass was among his papers.

– Okay. Out you get.

Me, I stand by the car, fear lapping at my brain. Moses, they handcuff.

– You follow in the car, boy.

I see Moses, head bent, as they steer him towards the back of the yellow van. His hands bound behind his back. His fingers clasped like fingers of an old man on a windy beach, eyes trawling the sand for flotsam or cowries. Let him go, I want to cry out. He is a beautiful man. But I am scared of the lancing blue eyes of the sarge and of the baying, caged dog. And of the rumour: they sjambok boys under 18 instead of jailing them like men. They tie you down. They gag your teeth before the sjambok flies. The sjambok, the flying boomslang that drops from overhead and fangs through your skin. And the sting is beyond the sting of clay flung from a kleilat. Or the sting of a cane. I pinch my fly to plug a spit of pee.

I follow behind the police van. The gears catch because I am so scared. We pull up outside a typical police station under a red zinc roof and a listless flag. I park next to the van. They leave Moses hunched in the back.

– Come inside, boy, the sarge says to me.

– Can I call my mother? I beg.

– If you are big enough to ferry illegal blacks around, you are big enough for a night in jail without holding your mama's hand.

– Jail?

– Just joking. We will get you back to your mama and you can suck her breast all you want. But we have to figure out what to do with the Bantu.

The typewriter zings as it reaches the end of a line.

– So, tell me your name.

– Douglas. Douglas Thomas.

⌒

Chaka barks. My mother comes running out onto the stoep.

– Douglas, are you hurt? What happened? she cries.

– They have Moses in the back because he has no pass.

– How could you lock an old man in the back of a van? she confronts the police.

The sarge shuffles his feet awkwardly.

– I am sorry, ma'am, we are just doing our duty. Illegal blacks are always hitching down to Cape Town, and there they squat in Crossroads.

– What do you intend to do with him?

– Well, ma'am. He has no pass. Under the law, we have no choice but to send him back to the Transkei. He is a Xhosa, is he not?

– He's a man, and you've caged him like an animal. His name is Moses and he's spent his life working down your goddamn mines. Now he's old and you want to exile him. No doubt you'd like to shoot him, like you would an old horse.

– Ma'am, we have a job to do.

– Look, I've seen his papers. They were in order.

My mother frowns at me because my gob is hanging open.

– It's not his fault his papers were stolen. And Pretoria has been slow to send him new papers. He's been a good gardenboy, captain.

– Sergeant, ma'am.

He glances at the other policeman. I have a feeling he would have been happy to be called captain had he been alone.

– Alright, ma'am, if you vouch for him, I'll let him go. But this is unusual procedure and could land me in trouble if it gets out.

– It won't get out. You have my word.

– Laat hom gaan, he mumbles.

The other policeman goes round to the back of the van. I hear the bolt slide, and then Moses comes out.

He bows his head to my mother.

– I'm sorry for the trouble, madam.

– Never mind. You go and lie down now.

He walks along the side of the house, past the kitchen steps, to the backyard khaya. The eyes of the policemen follow him, to make sure he does belong and is not going to scarper over the fence. He stops at the door. My heart beats. He reaches for the handle, as you do not knock at your own door. The door opens, though Hope remains unseen in the shadows. Moses goes inside.

– Perhaps your boy should stay put until his papers come, calls the sarge from the Land Rover window.

My mother waves and the Land Rover rumbles away.

Moses and Hope come out of Hope's khaya.

– Aai aai aai, goes Hope. I told you something bad would happen, madam. I told you.

– Hush now, Hope. How are you, Moses?

– I was a fool. Why would they let an old kaffir go down to Cape Town? Such a dream is just to dream.

– But Moses, we can go another way. Down the coast, past Port Elizabeth. Or through Montagu.

– Master Douglas, they are everywhere. If they do not catch me on the road, they will catch me in Cape Town. No, you go alone. I will stay here in this stone town.

– Moses, says my mother, if you want to, you can stay here and look after us, Hope and me. Hope, you can move inside.

– But, madam, the law forbids it.

– To hell with the law. Hope, you sleep in the spare room tonight.

go well

There is a gaping yearning in me to hold Moses, to nook my forehead in the hollow of his neck, to breathe him in. White yinyanged on black. Instead, we clasp hands.

– Go well, says Moses. You are a man.

– Stay well, Moses, I mouth.

Hope flaps about, full of foreboding that I will wind up dead if I go back to Muizenberg:

– The Langa skollies will kill you dead. Or the baboons.

My mother hugs me.

– You call me from Bessie's, or from a callbox, you hear.

As I climb into the Volvo, my mother has to prop Hope up, to keep her from flopping down to the grass. Chaka pees against the Volvo's tyres.

I reverse out of the yard.

– Don't forget to look up Johan Myburgh at the *Cape Times*, my mother calls after me. He'll give you a foot in the door.

Chaka chases the Volvo, biting at the tyres. My mother and Hope and Moses dwindle in the rearview mirror.

Chaka abandons the chase, his lolling pink tongue hangs out. I turn into the Shell to fill up.

There is a new Jim, wearing the overall with Jim sewn on the back. He is a wiry man and the overall looks flappy on him.

– Kunjani. Fill her up with 97.

While the pump runs up rands, Ou Piet Olifant lopes over from the Rhodes Hotel.

– Cape Town, hey my boy?

I nod.

– I thought so. Can I catch a ride?

I don't know what to say. This was the dream I shared with Moses.

– Just a joke, my boy. But I tell you, if District Six was still jiving, I would go for the show. Totsiens, my boy. Say howzit to Cape Town for me.

– Totsiens.

Clapton surfs a solo guitar riff on Radio 5 as I drive south out of Klipdorp, coral seeds in one pocket, Dodi's blood money in the other, Moses' dream in my head.

A few miles out, a hawk on a telegraph pole tilts an eye at me. Apart from random koppies and gullies and, sometimes, a koala gum shading a picnic spot, the veld is flat. It gives no hint of the mountains that will thrust up through the sand when I get to the Boland.

By nine the sun begins to burn and I imagine rockrabbits hiding under stones. Only the lizards stay out, etched like bushman paintings against stone.

I bite into a Granny Smith from the tuckbox of padkos Hope packed for me. Such apples they export overseas, to London and Amsterdam.

I squint out the sun as the road unwinds dizzily.

It begins to seep into my head that my tuckbox days are over and that I will have to find food alone.

I see a small buck on the peak of a distant koppie. A dikdik, or a duiker maybe. Or just a stray dog.

As I cross the vast veld under a pelting sun, images of Cape Town pop up in my head:

In front of the Harbour Café, seals scull lazily, their stomachs turned to the sun.

The patchwork of canvas-shaded stalls of Greenmarket Square.

The parrotfeather colours of the fishing boats in Hout Bay.

The Atlantic breaks against the Kalk Bay harbour wall. In the lagoon calm of the harbour, fish surface to nibble at red bait or bread crusts.

The compass hand of Cecil John Rhodes signposts the undiscovered hinterland northeast. Trek this tack over the mountains and through the Karoo and beyond, and you will find diamonds and gold.

⌒

The car gives up the ghost in Banhoek, on the hill beyond Pniel. I freewheel back down the hill to a sad, roadside garage. A cigarette stub dances in the corner of the mechanic's mouth as he mumbles his verdict.

– Engine's shot.

– Will you give me something for the car?

He smears grease on the bib of his overall and stares down the road to Pniel. I wonder if he has heard me.

– Is she worth anything?

– Two hundred rand, maybe.

– Two hundred rand?

– Might get something for the tyres.

I am glad Moses does not see me pocket the rand notes as dirty as a dipstick cloth. All the Sunday afternoons of tinkering under the hood or staring up at the diff, reduced to a few red notes.

I grab the duffelbag from the boot, and the Basotho blanket from the backseat, and walk uphill, lugging a heavy heart. I cannot bear to turn around. I know the yellow Volvo, jilted, abandoned, gazes her accusing headlights after me.

Further up the hill, I stop to buy hanepoot jam from a farm stall. I dip my finger into the hanepoot and lick it.

There is a dam just below the road, and the road bends around it. I climb through the fence and slither down the sandy slope to wash the stickiness away. The water is low and you can see the frame of a half-sunk bicycle. Three Egyptian geese glide further out, and watch me wash in water stained orange by the clay.

Back on the road, I thumb the cars that whine by. A blue Ford tractor rumbles along, towing a train of empty fruitbins that go *clatter, clatter clank*. The Egyptian geese beat the water with their wings, then fly over away towards the Simonsberg. I run after the tractor and jump onto the running-board of the trailer, the way the blacks do at dusk on Oom Jan's farm, after the last shift of fruitpicking. The driver turns around and waves me away. I just wave back at him. He shakes his head but drives on.

Sitting on the rim of a fruitbin, I watch the roadside pines go by and, behind the pines, the fruit Moses dreams of.

The tractor turns off the road just before Stellenbosch. I jump down and watch the tractor rattle out of sight along a dirt road.

I walk downhill on the rippling edge of the tar, past the bus depot and into the coloured quarter of Idas Valley.

I sit on the steps in front of the café in the afternoon sun, washing spicy samoosa down with neon-yellow Pinenut.

Then I walk to the crossroads, and I go up to cars when they stop at the light, the way beggars and newspaper boys do. A farmer in a bakkie says he can give me a ride as far as Spier, the wine farm.

– From there you can easy get a lift to Muizenberg.

It turns out he knows Oom Jan and that they once went fishing together in South West Africa.

At Spier, I stand by the side of the road. The train from Cape Town goes by: *kudu kudu kudu kudu kudu kudu kudu kudu.* I wave and the train whistles. Marsden and I sometimes rode this train from Cape Town to Stellenbosch, to spend a weekend with Dirkie.

An old Chev stops. It is a coloured family on their way to the beach. The father opens the boot to put the duffelbag inside, and beachbuckets and spades spill out. He gathers things again and ties down the boot with wire. The kids jump over the seat into the boot, and park on top of the bags and baskets and coolbox. They are going to the beach just this side of Sunrise we always drove past in Indlovu. I remember the colourful playground and braai spots the government built there for non-whites.

– They give us the beaches where the backwash is strong and where the sharks cruise up and down, up and down, the father laughs.

He drives past their beach to Sunrise Beach and drops me off by the fruitsellers. Then he U-turns and the kids wave through the back window as they head back.

The same fisherman is dodging motorcars and dangling his catch of snoek on the same spot. Four years of hawking snoek, come burning sun or howling southeaster. Four years of dancing on a compass foot while Muizenberg orbits round. Fours years of my drifting beyond the snoekseller's world, a world unaware of my exile, not batting an eyelid at my return.

I buy some grapes. A man wraps the fruit in brown paper.

– There you go, chief.

– I've come home, I tell him.

He nods. It is the only tangible thing to mark my homecoming.

– I've been away a long time.

– That's so, chief, that's so.

– Do you remember me?

– I remember you, chief. You and your brother, and the dog. Twins is not something you forget.

I feel ashamed that I do not remember him. I remember Byron and Matches, and the snoekseller, but the fruitsellers and lollyboys and paperboys and dustbinmen are just a blur of black faces in my mind.

– I was in the Karoo.

– I just know Cape Town, my basie.

– Well, see you, hey.

– See you, basie.

There are no sand yachts on the lot where we played cricket. I spit grape pips in the beach sand. I drop my shorts, not caring that I am wearing Jockeys rather than a Speedo, and run to the sea, the way Marsden and I used to run on my father's sandflicking heels. I dive as the tide sucks at my feet. It feels as if the cold will crush my skull. I surface and tread water. The cold gnaws into the bones in my feet, but I swim out to where the surfers ride the waves in rubber skins. Far away: the matchstick sunbathers and umbrella flowers.

– Chips, dude. We spotted a fin this morning.

– Thanks.

My heart pounds as I peer into the deep, shadowy water. Somewhere, down there, death lurks. A hint of the latent speed of an unshot torpedo in the casual flick of a tail. Gills rippling. Fine-tuned senses yearning for a rumour of blood. Chips, dude. Thanks for telling me, dude. Do I flap my hands and fly?

Though my fear tells me to freestyle ashore, I remember my

father's words: The thing to do is stay calm. Keep your feet under, and frogkick so the shark does not confuse your splashing feet for a wounded fish. If he homes in on you, you sink and stay down till he veers away. If he still wants you, go for his eyes. With sharks and ostriches, go for the eyes.

I realise I do not want to see the house, with other boys' bicycles on the grass and another maid on the kitchen steps.

☞

I paddle out through the ice-tea surf. The rising sun glints in the empty windows of the weekend train to Cape Town. I stand on a borrowed board. No flicks or tricks. The wave barrels. For a moment, I glide. Then the wave tumbles me. I fight it instead of going with it. Have I forgotten everything? I even forgot to dogleash the board to my foot. As I surface I hear the crack of the board on rock. I wade up out of the water, feeling ashamed.

The nose of the board is torn off and the fibreglass juts out rawly. I sit on the rocks by the broken board, the rocks where Venus came out of the sea. The rock pools are so clear I have to touch to be sure there is water there. A crab has burrowed under the damp sand and only his peppercorn eyes peer out. There is a smell of beached kelp rotting. Savvy seagulls hover above me. I feel sure they can smell the desert in me, Karoo boy.

☞

Dusk in Kalk Bay: I buy red bait and a handline and head for the harbour wall. The sun drops behind the mountain, orange and pink, like oil on the water.

I stare at the bobbing float, amid the dancing red and yellow reflections of the fishing boats and a dry seagull feather breezing over the water. In the rippling, lilting reflections I see my father's staring, unflinching eyes, lids peeled to bare white eyeballs.

It was not the ragged volley of Chaka's blunt barks that woke me that night in Muizenberg, four years ago. Nor the listless backyard rap of the other dogs of the neighbourhood. It was a tap on the skin of a tomtom, sent arrowing across the vast Karoo of black space behind my fluttering eyelids.

Though I am scared, I force myself to go on, out the kitchen door, out into the moon-bathed yard.

Hope's khaya is dark. She is visiting a boyfriend in Langa. Chaka abandons his barking when he sees me, wags his stump of a tail and grins white teeth in the moonlight. Crickets cheep cheep over the hazy hiss of the waves. Kamikaze moths orbit the streetlamp. My father's study door is ajar, leaking yellow glow onto the grass. There is no sound from his study. No tapping of typewriter keys. No Miles Davis or Steely Dan.

I feel Chaka's hot breath on my calf as the door fans open.

Then my mind fades to black. All the Karoo years long, the spooled images lay in a far dark zone of my mind: latent with memory, yet undeveloped.

Now the images float out of the dark into a lagoon of consciousness:

My father's gaping eyes.

His blood pooling glutinously as sump oil around his head, across the desk, tinging the typed pages of his unfinished novel.

A bindi of blood on the forehead of the Venus de Milo.

A zizzing fly swimming in the bottle of Jack Daniel's.

The black gun on the floor, stumpy as a cold black toad.

A tug at the line jerks me back to reality. Bollard reality. The float dives. I wind the gut onto the reel. A seagull caws hopefully.

But the fish jigs free. Damn. I have lost the feel for it. I forgot to yank the line so the hook bites deep into the gills. I reel in. The hook is bare of bait.

Again, I stand by my mother on the Kalk Bay harbour wall, twinless boy of fourteen. Again, wind dusts ashes from my mother's hands, to a soundtrack of seagull cries and muffled voices and radio-static surf. But this other sinking of ash and flower among yawning fish is just a dream, a déjà vu. My flirting, finger-tapping, snake-catching father is not dead, he has just sailed away, up the east coast of Africa, to a place where lions run on the beach. A place where you can write a novel.

I ditch the rest of the red bait into the water. Fish dart at it as it sinks, as they arrowed in on the ashes of a man who dreamed his boys would one day play cricket for the province, the ashes of a head islanded in blood.

I turn my pocket out, and empty the orange coral seeds into the harbour. Lucky beads. Fish surface and, with a flick of fin, swallow an unhooked seed.

Tomorrow I will ride the train into Cape Town and look up Johan Myburgh, my father's old friend on the newspaper. Perhaps he will find a job for me as coffee boy, the way my father began.

Author's Note
Though the Hard Rock Cafe in Sea Point did not exist in 1976,
I whimsically shifted it along the timeline of my mind.
You will find Muizenberg on the map of South Africa,
but Klipdorp is a fictive echo of all the boondock dorps
in the bleak Karoo hinterland of South Africa.

Thanks to:
Daniela, for her intuition. Mia, for her magical laughter.
My folks, for my childhood in Africa. My brother, Dean, for all
the frontyard cricket. Tarryn, whose fleeting life was a fiery poem.
Finn Spicer, James Scorer, Tom de Fonblanque,
Andrew Macdonald, for reading my novel pencil in hand.
Gillian Warren-Brown, Jørgen Heramb, Neil Wetmore,
Conrad K., Zane Godwin, Nigel Gwynne-Evans, Andrew Stooke,
Tim Volem, Meg Foster, Geoff Roberts, Leon Kandelaars,
William Siegfried, for their faith. Alan Paton, for the words
which awoke in me the desire to write of Africa. Delarey, beyond
the horizon. Emil Holzinger, for the chance to read this novel to
life on a hill above Vienna. Isobel Dixon, for her skilled eye and
narrative instinct. All my students through the years.

Troy Blacklaws was born in 1965 in Pinetown. When he was nine, his family moved from Natal to the Cape, to a wine farm at the foot of the Simonsberg. He attended Paarl Boys' High. His world seemed natural until he discovered the truth: that apartheid South Africa was a world pariah and that he had been hoodwinked. After school, he studied literature at Rhodes University. He then spent two bitter years in the army before teaching English in East London. In 1993 he went to England and taught at Stowe, north of Oxford, and Sherborne, in Dorset. Since 1996 he has taught at international schools in Vienna and Frankfurt.